Robert Young

Trophies from African Heathenism

Robert Young

Trophies from African Heathenism

ISBN/EAN: 9783742810632

Manufactured in Europe, USA, Canada, Australia, Japa

Cover: Foto ©Andreas Hilbeck / pixelio.de

Manufactured and distributed by brebook publishing software
(www.brebook.com)

Robert Young

Trophies from African Heathenism

TROPHIES

FROM

AFRICAN HEATHENISM

BY

ROBERT YOUNG, F.R.S.G.S.

Author of
"Modern Missions," "Light in Lands of Darkness," and
"The Success of Christian Missions"

WITH MAP

London
HODDER AND STOUGHTON
27, PATERNOSTER ROW

MDCCCXCII.

Butler & Tanner,
The Selwood Printing Works,
Frome, and London.

PREFATORY NOTE.

WITH nearly all of those whose cases are here narrated, it was my privilege to have more or less personal intercourse. In so far as the information thus obtained was defective, owing to my limited opportunities, as it could hardly fail to be, it has been supplemented by friends, clerical and lay, who were conversant with the facts. To all such I beg to tender my grateful acknowledgments.

Though I had the pleasure of visiting the stations of various churches and societies, these visits were mostly of too casual a nature to permit of my becoming acquainted with particular cases, such as was vouchsafed to me in connection especially with the Missions of the Free Church of Scotland.

I would willingly aid in perpetuating the memory of the noble men who laid the foundations of the Christian Church in South Africa—the names, in particular, of Schmidt, Lemmertz, and Hoffman of the Moravian Missions; Vanderkemp, Philip,

Campbell, Williams, Moffat, Livingstone, Brownlee, Calderwood, Birt, and Mackenzie of the London Missionary Society; Gray, Callaway, and Taberer of the Propagation Society; Shaw (Barnabas and William), Shepstone, and Appleyard of the Wesleyan Missionary Society; Adams, Lindley, Grout, and Tyler of the American Board; Thomson, Bennie, Ross, Chalmers, Weir, Macdiarmid, Laing, Govan, Cumming, and Allison of the Free and United Presbyterian Churches of Scotland; Pellissier, Casalis, and Coillard of the Paris Missionary Society; Dohne, Posselt and his son from the Berlin Mission; Creux and Berthoud from the Canton de Vaud; Schrueder from the Norwegian Missionary Society. Such names deserve to be held in loving and lasting remembrance.

The author hopes the admirable Map by Messrs. Bartholomew & Co., may prove useful. The want of such an aid in books in which places are described has often been felt. Thus Sir Walter Scott, in thanking Southey for his "History of Brazil," says,—"There is only one defect I can point out—I mean the want of a good map. For, to tell you the truth, with my imperfect atlas of

South America, I can hardly trace these same *Tups* of yours (which in our border dialect signifies *rams*), with all their divisions and sub-divisions, through so many ramifications, without a *carte de pays*."

The following "Short and Simple Annals" of a few members of the African race are sent forth with the prayer that they may be accompanied by the Divine blessing, and in the hope that the same generous consideration shown by the Press in connection with my previous publications will be extended to me in the present instance.

R. Y.

2, MERCHISTON PLACE,
EDINBURGH, *July*, 1892.

CONTENTS.

"O Africa! long lost in night,
Upon the horizon gleams the light
Of breathing dawn. Thy star of fame
Shall rise and brightly gleam: thy name
Shall blaze in history's later page;
Thy birth-time is the last great age:
Thy name has been, Slave of the world;
But, when thy banner is unfurled,
Triumphant liberty shall wave
That standard o'er foul slavery's grave,
And earth, decaying earth shall see
Her freest, fairest child in thee."

"The people that walked in darkness have seen a great light: they that dwelt in the land of the shadow of death, upon them hath the light shined."—ISA. ix. 2 (R.V.).

INTRODUCTION.

NATURE in its boundless aspects and variety is best seen and appreciated, and a truer estimate is formed of it, when looked at by way of contrast. Thus spring, under the genial influence of refreshing rain and sunshine, when trees and plants burst afresh into life, is hailed the more gladly because it succeeds the blasts and frosts of winter, when all is shrouded in gloom, and the entire vegetable world *seems*, but *only* seems, to have had the sentence of death passed upon it. In like manner, the pleasure of the bright cheery months of summer in their holiday attire is enhanced, following as they do those that bring with them not only fresh new life, but also the keen, bitter winds that prove so trying to the invalid, especially in the more exposed districts of our native land. So, too, the clear blue sky and calm of ocean are never more thoroughly enjoyed by landsmen than when they succeed the dark overhanging clouds, and howling winds, and storm-tossed billows. It is the same in human life. Calling on an invalid lady one bright summer afternoon, I found she had just returned from a drive, her first outing after two years' confinement to a sick chamber. Much as I enjoyed being out in such genial weather, the enjoyment in *her* case could not fail to be greatly heightened. The principle holds good all round. I propose in these introductory remarks to apply it to the subject in hand, looking at the present condition of the missionary enterprise in South Africa in the light of the past.

Forty years ago—not to go further back—the interest in African Missions, so far at least as the Free Church of Scotland was concerned, stood nearly at zero, being then confined for the most part to the *western* towns and districts, from which the early missionaries went forth.[1] The Church

[1] These missionaries were—Rev. W. R. Thomson and Rev. John Bennie, 1821; Rev. John Ross, 1823; Rev. Wm. Chalmers, Messrs. James Weir and Alexander McDiarmid,

in that part of the country, in its efforts to plant the standard of the Cross in Africa, received but scant recognition and help from the Church at large. Not only so: when several years previously (1849) the missions of that Church were feeling the pressure of financial difficulty, a proposal on the part of the Foreign Missions Committee to curtail the sphere of their operations by practically abandoning the work in that field was seriously entertained, and it was mainly owing to the representations and remonstrances of the friends in the West that more enlightened counsels prevailed.

The Free Church of Scotland was not alone in its lack of missionary interest in that part of the world. The Rev. James A. Hewitt, in his volume of "Sketches of English Church History in South Africa," remarks:

"Though England has now held possession of the Cape for more than forty years, the mother Church had evinced very little interest in the religious condition of South Africa,

---

1827; Rev. James Laing, 1830; Rev. Robert Niven, 1836; and Rev. Wm. Govan, 1840.

which, though nominally under the spiritual charge of the Bishop of Calcutta, was (until 1848) in as neglected and hopeless a state as could well be . . . The S.P.G. was spending in Africa £75 out of the annual income of £89,000; and the whole amount raised by the Church in the Colony was not more than £500 a year. There were twelve chaplains, at a cost to Government of £2,945 a year, and two others supported by the Colonial Church Society. . . . Nor was any attempt made to gather into the Church's fold the multitudes of heathen with whom the Colony abounded. While English, French, and German societies of various denominations were sending out their missionaries, the Church of England was almost the only communion which was doing nothing for the conversion of the heathen within and around the Colony . . ."

But to return: Instead of a backward, suicidal movement, the Free Church, after due consideration, decided to advance in the direction of securing an enlarged revenue, and so of maintaining and, if possible, extending the work. And although the advance for some years thereafter, like the flow of some of the South African rivers, was sluggish enough, it has been from the time of Livingstone's published explorations, and especially since his death, more marked and on the whole steady and satisfactory, notwithstanding occasional checks from wars and other causes.

And what is still more to the point, the interest is no longer confined to the western districts, but is co-extensive with the Church's bounds. It is however still wanting in pervasiveness and depth.

How stands the case? Forty years ago the Free Church of Scotland—it is singled out simply by way of illustration, and because the writer is familiar with the facts—forty years ago, that Church, whose sphere of action in the African field was at the time confined within very narrow limits, had only three principal and fifteen or thereby out-stations in Kafirland, under the care of four ordained and two lay missionaries, along with three female European teachers. *Now*, besides Kafirland South, its operations have been extended to Kafirland North, beyond the Great Kei river, into Tembuland, East Griqualand, Natal, from the southern shores to the upper end of Lake Nyassa, and even much further to the north of East Central Africa, on the banks of the Kibwezi, where Dr. Stewart has successfully laid the foundations of another Lovedale. The field embraces in Cape Colony and Natal alone a native population of 1,650,000 souls.[1] Leaving out of view the new Lovedale, which is still only in the formative process, there are in the other fields 13 principal and 125 out-stations, under the superintendence of 73 European agents, of whom 20 are ordained missionaries, 17 male and 19 female teachers, and 17 artizan evangelists, or, reckoning also native labourers, 292 Christian agents in all.

Again, forty years ago, the number in full communion at the several stations of the Free Church in Kafirland was rather less than 100, and the pupils under Christian instruction were slightly over 200. *Now*, the numbers in the various fields are respectively, 4,726 and 9,304.

[1] The following statistics are taken from a recent issue of the *Journal des Missions Evangeliques*:—

	Native Population.	Baptized.	Communicants.
Cape Colony	1,148,930	229,435	42,363
Natal	500,000	22,454	6,300
Basutoland	268,500	17,800	5,700
Bechuanaland	7,000	900	300
Transvaal...	100,000	33,763	14,095
Orange Free State ...	129,000	15,098	4,323
Totals	2,455,030	349,360	73,084

The ratio of progress too will be seen by a comparison of the numbers at the close of the last five decades, thus :—

	Communicants.	Pupils.
For 1851 there were returned	100	210
„ 1861 „ „	577	748
„ 1871 „ „	1,250	1,480
„ 1881 „ „	2,318	3,104
„ 1891 „ „	4,726	9,304

The total number who have been admitted to the membership of the Church on a profession of their faith in Christ since the commencement of the missions of the Free Church in Africa is not fewer than 8,450.

It may be added that at the close of 1891 there were 661 candidates for baptism, and that the natives contributed during the year for buildings and the support of ordinances £950, besides £3,285 in the shape of school fees.

These figures indicate progress—not such progress, it is true, as one could have desired; but still, having regard to the feeble efforts put forth by friends at home, and to the hindrances on the part of others, sufficient to show that solid work is being done, and that it has been attended in the past by an encouraging measure of success. Whatever others may think of it, the fact that 8,450 Africans have been detached from heathenism and enrolled among the disciples of Christ—not to speak of other and more indirect benefits—through the instrumentality of one single branch of the Christian Church, ought to be matter for profound thankfulness and praise to God over all.

It is not my purpose in these pages to trace the progress and beneficial influence and results of any particular mission, or of the missions as a whole in that part of the world. A few remarks on the general subject is all that is contemplated. My object is of a less pretentious nature. It is to concentrate attention specially, though not exclusively, on one aspect of the mission work there, namely, its *genuineness*, as seen in the changed lives of some of the more notable of the converts.

When Moses sent representatives of the tribes to spy out the land of Canaan, the majority, while testifying to the goodness of the land, as they could hardly fail to do, in view of the clusters of grapes, pomegranates, etc., which they had carried with them from Eshcol, at the same time brought back an unfavourable report of its inhabitants. In consequence, the people were so discouraged that they not only murmured against Moses and Aaron, but even went the length of proposing to appoint a captain who might lead them back to Egypt. It was otherwise with Joshua and Caleb—faithful among the faithless—the latter stilling the people and urging them to go up at once and possess the land, as they were well able to overcome it. For, added the two faithful witness-bearers, notwithstanding the strength of the Canaanites, and the walled cities in which they dwelt, "their defence is removed from over them, and the Lord is with us; fear them not."—Num. xiv. 9 (R.V.).

The history has its counterpart in South Africa. There is a general consensus of opinion as to the goodness of the land, its healthy climate and immense mineral and other resources and capabilities, needing only the introduction of capital, the extension of the railway system, the making of more roads and bridges, a more extensive and perfect system of irrigation and other appliances, in order to the development of the country. But as regards the *inhabitants* of the land, there are those even within the pale of the Christian Church who would leave them alone in their barbarism, and who are in the habit of making comparisons between the *red* heathen and the educated and Christianised native, and usually to the disparagement of the latter. Yet is it undoubtedly the will of God, as revealed in His Word, that the natives of South Africa—I might rather say of every part of the world—should not be left in their heathenism, but that they should be raised from their degradation, Christianised, saved. And this is exactly what the various sections of the Christian Church are endeavouring to do, according to the best light they possess and the resources at their command.

I plead that each man and woman who makes a Christian profession is under law to Christ to aid in evangelising the heathen, and I back up my plea by quoting to those who treat the matter with studied and systematic indifference and neglect the words of the four conscience-stricken lepers at the gate of Samaria: "We do not well; for this day is a day of good tidings, and we hold our peace" (2 Kings vii. 9).

Nor will such as stand aloof free themselves of responsibility by attempts to fasten on the shoulders of the missionaries whatever is blameworthy either in their own conduct or in that of native Christians, as if the inconsistencies and shortcomings of others could ever form a valid excuse for the neglect of a plain command. It may be readily admitted that the missionaries are not all that might be desired in respect of character and the other qualities that one expects to find in them, and that their work is not free from those blemishes and mistakes that mar its usefulness. The best among them will be the readiest to acknowledge that they are after all earthen vessels, with more or less earthliness adhering to them. Many of them, I am sure, will heartily re-echo the remarks recently made by a Bengal missionary :—[1]

"We all," he said, "are feeling it, and many are saying it, that our chief need now in India is a more thorough and

---

[1] James L. Phillips, M.A., M.D., at the Calcutta Missionary Conference, May 11th, 1891.

sustained spiritual equipment. Very thankful indeed am I for the privilege of coming back to my own beloved Bengal, to work with you here, and I have come with the prayer in my heart that I might do more for my Lord, that I might do it better, and that all of us might see the way to do more and learn the way to do better in the work to which God has called us." And again, "There are our critics. They have freely criticised missionary manners, missionary methods, and sometimes missionary motives as well. I say it sincerely, I thank God for the critics. Let them search us and our work through and through, and let them speak out boldly. Either their carelessness or our blundering will be sure to appear, and good must come of it. Our work is open to inspection on every side, and I would not have it otherwise. . . ."

What I desire to emphasize in connection with the elevation of the natives is, that while commercial, industrial, and other undertakings, promoted by companies or by the Government, have an important part to play, and while all such enterprises are to be hailed with satisfaction, and as far as possible encouraged by substantial aid, no permanently satisfactory result can be looked for unless they are accompanied by the dissemination among the people of the gospel message and the Christian education of the young, combined with industrial training. These, after all, are the most important factors in the moulding of the national character. For, as her Majesty Queen Victoria, in a letter to some African chiefs, well and truly put it, "Commerce alone will not make a nation great and happy. England has been great and happy by the knowledge of the true God and of Jesus Christ."

Among the many who have devoted their energies in promoting the welfare of the natives, it will not, I trust, be considered invidious to refer here to the important services rendered by Sir George Grey. No one certainly had more enlightened views and a clearer perception of what was necessary, or laboured more indefatigably in order to secure the moral subjugation of the various South African races. All through the seven years during which he held the high office of Governor of the Cape of Good Hope, his aim was, by teaching and encouraging the natives, to improve their condition, and gradually making them—to quote his own words—"a part of ourselves, with a common faith and common interests; useful servants, consumers of our goods, contributors to our revenues; in short, a source of strength and wealth to the colony, such as Providence designed them to be." [1]

Not less worthy of special note are the sympathy, sagacity, and helpful aid of Sir Langham Dale,[2] the able Superintendent-General of Education, in connection with the amelioration of the native races. In particular, he aims at introducing between the ordinary day school and the factory or industrial department what he terms the trade school, in which a competent knowledge of various industries might be obtained by both sexes at moderate cost. His views may be gathered from the following statement :—

"The only available agencies for transforming the native savage into a citizen, capable of understanding his duties and of fulfilling them, are the school, the workshop, and the Christian Church. I wish to cultivate together the brain and the hand ; the teaching, intellectual and moral, of the Church and of the School, needs, as I have said, an industrial *substratum* in its disciples ; true Christianity is incompatible with the aimlessness of savage life ; the pith of the Christian life is in the will and the means to be doing. What can be the outcome of all the teaching, religious and secular, if recipients are left to the unrestrained license and apathetic indolence of a mode of living that makes no

---

[1] "South Africa—Past and Present," p. 72.

[2] Now retired, and is succeeded by Thomas Muir, LL.D., F.R.S.E.

account of the responsibility of man, and offers no sphere for self-improvement, much less for self-control, which is the basis of morality?" [1]

These are weighty words, and well deserve to be pondered, coming as they do from one who has had a lengthened and varied experience. Some progress has been made towards the realization of the ideal sketched by both of the foregoing authorities; but the problem has to be worked out on a greatly enlarged scale.

It has been my privilege once and again to traverse a considerable portion of the South African continent, and to mark the social, moral, and spiritual effects resulting directly and indirectly from missionary labour.

A century ago, and less, little was known of the interior of even that portion of the country, while the extensive lake region further to the north was so completely a *terra incognita* that one is reminded of Dean Swift's witty lines:—

> "So geographers in Afric maps
> With savage pictures fill their gaps,
> And o'er unhabitable downs
> Place elephants instead of towns."

[1] Lovedale *Christian Express* for March, 1892, p. 46.

But during the latter half of the present century the country has been so thoroughly explored, speaking generally, that something at least is now known of its main features, and the extent to which it is peopled by multitudinous tribes. And as regards *South* Africa in particular, it is no longer, as in Vanderkemp's day, when he pitched his tent at Bethelsdorp, near Port Elizabeth, and afterwards under a well-known tree in the neighbourhood of Pirie station, a vast unbroken moral wilderness. On the contrary, one sees in all directions, at distances ranging roughly from ten or twelve to twenty or thirty miles, the mission stations of the Germans (Berlin, Rhenish, or Hermannsburg Societies), the Moravians, the French, the Swedish, the Swiss, the American Board, the Church of England, the Wesleyans, the London Missionary Society, the Free and United Presbyterian Churches of Scotland, or others, each a centre from which the light of gospel truth is being diffused, and each able to show a record of success achieved. And although the mass of the people is still confessedly heathen, and extensive portions of the country, as in Tembuland, Pondoland and Zululand, are still unoccupied by any Church or Society, the work accomplished during the past seventy years may be accepted as an earnest of a still greater ingathering in the not distant future. Each station visited or seen in the distance had always to me the appearance of an *oasis*, the tall, graceful blue gums usually surrounding it being a suitable emblem of those "trees of righteousness, the planting of the Lord, that He might be glorified," which it is the chief design of the missions to raise up.

Having brought back with me from that goodly land an Eshcol cluster of the spiritual fruit reaped by the missionaries there, I now submit it to the reader. The "sketches" are to be regarded simply as specimens. There is not one of the numerous missionaries in the field who could not, if desired, produce a similar or even larger cluster than what these pages contain.

One of the ideas underlying the book has been well expressed by Dr. Alex. Maclaren, of Manchester, as follows :—

"To talk about hundreds of millions of idolaters leaves the heart untouched. But take one soul out of all that mass, and try to feel what his life is in its pitchy darkness, broken only by lurid lights of fear and sickly gleams of hope, in its passions ungoverned by love, its remorse uncalmed by pardon, its affections feeling like the tendrils of some climbing plant for the stay they cannot find, and in the cruel blackness that swallows it up irrevocably at last. Follow him from the childhood that knows no discipline to the grave that knows no waking, and will not the solitary instance come nearer our hearts than the millions?"[2]

It is to be hoped that this will be the effect produced by the "solitary instances" here narrated, the more so that the individual lives thus portrayed do not end in "pitchy darkness," but are destined on the resurrection morn to emerge, under the all-powerful influence of the Divine Spirit, into the glorious light and liberty that characterize the ransomed of the Lord, who, it is said, "shall return, and come with singing unto Zion; and everlasting joy shall be upon their heads."—Isa. xxxv. 10 (R.V.).

[2] From "The Secret of Power," and other sermons. (Macmillan & Co., 1882.)

OLD SUTU:

A LONG LIFE WITH A GRAND ENDING.

" *Verily my house is not so with God: yet He hath made with me an everlasting covenant, ordered in all things, and sure: for it is all my salvation.*"—2 SAM. xxiii. 5 (R.V.).

OLD SUTU:

A LONG LIFE WITH A GRAND ENDING.

THE name of old Sutu was for many long years a household word among the Kafirs. Old Sutu was the principal or "great" wife of Gaika, who as paramount chief ruled for a lengthened period over some 80,000 Kafirs. According to established custom, he chose her, not from his own, but from a different tribe—the Tambookies. On the occasion of their marriage he appointed Kamé, one of his numerous secondary wives, to wait upon her, as her future companion, in which position she was eminently faithful, even unto death.

After Gaika's death, in November, 1829, his son Sandilli being then young, Sutu acted as queen-regent, and discharged the duties of her station with such ability as to win the respect and reverence of the entire tribe. She was justly regarded as a remarkable woman in her day, and had many varied and trying experiences. She waged a long struggle between the best missionary influences and the worst influences of heathenism, and it was not until many long years had elapsed that the latter yielded to the former. One or two incidents in her eventful and chequered life may be noted.

For a number of years Sutu resided with her son Sandilli at the "Great Place," as the residence of the chief is called, on the higher ridge above the mission church and native kraals at Burnshill. During her regency, until Sandilli was of age, Macomo,[1] the eldest son of Gaika by a *secondary* wife, formed a plot to get rid of Sutu, in order that he might become regent, and so ultimately succeed to the chieftainship. Accordingly, when in 1842 Tyali, another of Gaika's sons, died, Macomo influenced the witch doctor to lay the charge of his sickness and death upon Sutu. Had it succeeded, she would have been condemned to be burnt. Happily for her, it came to the ears of the

[1] Macomo, though Gaika's eldest son, was, according to Kafir custom, subordinate to Sandilli, the son of the chief's "great" wife.

dying man, whereupon he sent a messenger secretly to Mr. Stretch, the diplomatic agent, to say that he had full confidence in Sutu's innocence, and that Macomo was seeking her destruction. Hearing also that Sutu was on her way to visit him in his sickness, Tyali sent to warn her of her danger, and to advise her to return to the "Great Place," where she would be in safety. In the meantime Mr. Stretch warned Macomo that if he attempted to carry out his deadly plot he would bring all the power of the Government to crush him. This warning had the desired effect. When Tyali died, not a finger was lifted up against Sutu.

Again, in a hut close by where Sutu lived at Burnshill, Tente, yet another of Gaika's sons, also lay a-dying. He was among the first to be admitted as a pupil to the Lovedale Institution at its opening in 1841, where he remained until the outbreak of the war in 1846. After his conversion he was for a number of years a highly valued teacher at one of the out-stations of the Burnshill Mission.

When near his end it came to Tente's knowledge that a report was abroad that, according to the Kafir custom as regards chiefs, the Kafir doctor had authority to smell out the person who had bewitched him and was the cause of his illness, and that his own wife had been fixed on as the victim. Putting his hand to his mouth, in Kafir fashion, Tente said in amazement,—

"How can people invent such things? It is well known that I have long given up all confidence in witch-doctors, and opposed them as much as I was able."

Inquiring what in the circumstances he ought to do, it was suggested that he might make a declaration in the presence of the chiefs. He accordingly asked two of the native teachers to go to the "Great Place" and request Sutu and Sandilli to come, as he had something to communicate to them.

In about two hours Sutu arrived with a considerable number of people. When all were seated Tente, who was rapidly sinking, asked to be raised up in his bed, and then audibly and distinctly, though with difficulty, made the following declaration:—

"My friends, I have called you to speak with

you before I die. You know the service in which I have been engaged, and that I have long come out from among your ways and customs. Christ is my Physician. I have given up all confidence in human skill and medicine, whether administered by the teachers or the Kafir doctors, and if any word contrary to this shall come out after my death, you chiefs will know it to be untrue. And if you shall do anything at the station after my death (referring to the smelling out and plundering after Kafir custom) you must not say it was on my account, but for your own covetousness."

Sutu inquired from what quarter the report had come.

Tente replied, not from the "Great Place," but, pointing towards the west, he said, from that quarter, but that he did not wish to be more particular. Then in an emphatic and most impressive manner he declared that the Word of God was great, that his views of it were unchanged, and that his dying wish was that they might all embrace it, adding—"It is now time for church." To the church accordingly the assembled natives repaired, Sutu, Sandilli, and other chiefs being among the number.

Tente's dying testimony made a deep impression, and not least upon Sutu, who a few days afterwards accompanied his remains to the mission burying-ground.

Sutu was always friendly to the missionaries, receiving them kindly at the "Great Place," and listening respectfully to their instructions. When Sandilli came of age and had entered on the chieftainship, he revived an ancient wicked custom, greatly to the grief of Sutu as well as of the missionaries. At that time the missionaries met at Burnshill for prayer and conference. It was agreed to proceed in a body and remonstrate with Sandilli respecting the matter. They reached the "Great Place," where Sutu received them kindly; but it was some time before Sandilli made his appearance. At length he emerged from the door of his hut with a large marrow-bone in his hand. The Rev. Henry Calderwood, long a missionary of the London Missionary Society, and in later years Civil Commissioner for the district of Victoria, in the Eastern province of the Cape of Good Hope, was the mouthpiece of the missionary band, who stood by him in front of the hut. While the speaker was earnestly expatiating on the evil consequences of the custom complained of, Sandilli would lift up the bone to his mouth and tug at the piece of flesh still adhering to it ; or, if too tough for his teeth, he would apply his assegai with the one hand while he held the bone with the other, his eyes at the same time glaring at the speaker and then at his supporters, as if they wished to deprive him of his fondly relished enjoyment. At length the speaker stopped, when Sandilli, inquiring if *that* was all, said, " I have heard you," and turning round, plunged into the hut and disappeared. The scene must have been ludicrous enough in one aspect of it, but disappointing and even humiliating in another. So doubtless it would appear to the missionaries as they retraced their steps to the Mission House.

As age and experience however advanced, Sandilli greatly improved. And no feature of his character was more remarkable than his attachment to his mother. When the war of 1877 broke out he came to Mr. Cumming, the venerable and much-respected missionary of the United Presbyterian Church at Emgwali, and sitting down, he said "he had just come from a meeting of his counsellors, and was quite opposed to taking part in the war. But," he added, "if it should happen that I am driven into war, what shall I do with my mother?" Stretching out his leg, "See," he went on to ask, "can I run with such a leg, or, if hunted among the rocks, how shall I protect my mother? Mfundis, will you look after her?" "Certainly," Mr. Cumming replied; "let her come to the station, and I shall see what can be done for her."

Leaving her home about three miles distant, Sutu, as arranged by Sandilli, in due time appeared at Emgwali, dressed in her red-ochred skin kaross, with petticoats of the same material. She took up her abode in the hut prepared for her, the school people doing everything in their power to make her comfortable. She was accompanied by her daughter, a fine, stately-looking widow, along with Kamé, her inseparable companion and friend.

All the cows given by Sandilli for Sutu's support were carried off in the raids of the enemy. But her wants were in one way and another supplied; and in response to an application by Mr.

Cumming on her behalf, the Government granted her a pension of a shilling a day for life. Thus she was to some extent provided for, though the provision was confessedly to the last degree meagre for one who had once been mistress of Kafirland.

Mr. Cumming had visited Sutu's kraal on the banks of the Kabousé, and held service there, on which occasions she invariably called upon all in the place to attend. And now at length, when settled in peace and in a measure of comfort at Emgwali, the truth seemed to be working in her heart. The first indication of this was that her leathern garments were soon cast off, and that a dress becoming her new circumstances was adopted. Then, although distant about a mile from the church, she, with her daughter and Kamé, were Sabbath after Sabbath generally found amongst the first to arrive, waiting to take part in the services of the day. In due time they were all enabled to make a public profession of their faith in Christ. Makazi, her daughter, was the first to be received into the fellowship of the Church; then Sutu, and lastly, Kamé. This was in 1880, Sutu being at the time about ninety years of age and blind.

At all the prayer-meetings held in the village in which Sutu lived—for there are five villages connected with Emgwali station—she was unfailing in her attendance. When Sandilli, her son, who had joined in the rebellion, was killed, she mourned for him, but never murmured. Though reduced from the highest position in the tribe to one of the lowest dependence, she was always cheerful and contented. She was possessed of great calmness and dignity of manner. And Mr. Cumming testifies that she grew in grace amazingly. Love to the Lord Jesus was a favourite theme of conversation.

One other sore trial Sutu had to bear as a Christian in her old age: Dundas, her only other son, lived on the station during the war, but followed the heathen part of the people when they crossed the Kei. He is said to have been a thoroughly selfish man, and, what is far worse, heartless. Though comparatively rich in cattle, he never once gave his mother the slightest help. When he and some of the chief men who had crossed the Kei with him were appealed to by Mr. Cumming to supply Sutu, the real sovereign of the tribe, with a cow, to help her in her straitened circumstances, their reply was, "If she will leave the school and come and live with us, as before, then we will help her, but not otherwise." Sutu, however, preferred to remain at Emgwali, in the possession of her Christian privileges.

The Rev. George Carstairs, of Glasgow, having visited her in 1883, he inquired what she had to say about the Lord Jesus. The blind eyes, he states, seemed to blaze, and the aged frame to gather its whole force, as she replied, "I love Jesus." Mr. Carstairs said, "You have had great losses: you have lost your husband, Gaika; you have lost your son, Sandilli; you have lost your country; you have lost your people; you have lost your property; and now you have lost your sight; but you have found more than all you have lost, if you have found Jesus." Her eyes filled with tears, and her face, it is said, beamed with delight as she replied, "I forget all my losses. I do not think of them. I think of what I have found in Jesus, and

I am satisfied." A hymn having been sung she fairly broke down, and said, " I cannot sing, but my heart sings."

Old Sutu felt like the reckless betting man, who had lost £165 at the Epsom racecourse, and was returning penniless and miserable into Epsom town, when he stopped to listen to an open-air preacher, was made to feel himself a lost and ruined sinner, and there and then closed with the gospel offer. In relating his experience, he said, " I had lost £165, but I went home to my wife and children richer than I came, for I had found Christ."

Accompanied by Mr. Cumming, it was my privilege to visit Sutu in 1885. I found her seated on a mat on the earthen floor of her hut, contented and happy. Beside her was Kamé, who, as maid of honour, had been her warmly attached friend during the fifty-five years of her widowhood. It was a beautiful and touching sight to see these two aged and now Christian Kafir women patiently waiting until the Lord should see meet to call them home.

Old Sutu died some months after my visit. As

she approached the termination of her ninety-five years' pilgrimage, Mr. Cumming inquired how she now felt regarding the Saviour. Lifting her head from her pillow, she exclaimed with great fervour, "I love my Lord greatly." Soon after she passed gently away, leaving behind her many precious memories. Indeed, when at any time in addressing the heathen, Sutu's conversion was referred to, it never failed to command attention, and to leave a deep impression.

Sutu's remains were interred in the neighbouring native cemetery, amidst the sorrowings of those who attended her funeral.

This sketch would be wanting in completeness without a closing reference to Kamé. She was no doubt greatly influenced by Sutu's superior mental abilities and Christian example. After the death of the latter it was pleasing to find how she awakened to a sense of her situation, and how she seemed to assume somewhat of Sutu's character. She felt her loss, and longed to follow her mistress and friend, to whom she had been so devotedly attached, and whom she so faithfully served. Her wishes were ere long gratified, for within a year she too had passed away to join her beloved Sutu in praising Him who had called them both out of darkness into His marvellous light.

KAFIR DEVOTION IN TIME OF WAR.

"Shall I drink the blood of the men that went in jeopardy of their lives? therefore he (David) would not drink it"—2 SAM. xxiii. 17 (R.V.).

KAFIR DEVOTION IN TIME OF WAR.

SELFISHNESS, which is everywhere inherent in fallen human nature, has found in the heathen Kafir congenial soil, and is indeed one of his most striking characteristics. He has been described as the "very incarnation of selfishness." Thus the Rev. Henry Calderwood, already referred to, mentions that during a famine (a very frequent occurrence in South Africa, owing to long continued droughts), an English lady took into her house a poor famished Kafir woman, reduced to a state of the greatest weakness and helplessness. The starving woman was by her fed and cared for. When able for work again her benefactress requested her to take a pail and fetch some water for household purposes, when she coolly asked, "What will you pay me?" Even the converts of the missions are far from being free of this vice in its grosser forms.

The picture has, however, a bright side. One instance among many may here be furnished, showing the power of the gospel when received into the heart in subduing this inborn selfishness. The facts were supplied by Mr. Calderwood.

During the Kafir War of 1846, when his beautiful station of Birklands, along with almost every other station in Kafirland, was destroyed by the Kafirs, and there seemed little hope of the country getting soon again into a settled condition, Mr. Calderwood resolved to return, for a time at least, to his native land. With this view he proceeded to Grahamstown, where he met some Christian friends, who expressed themselves as strongly opposed to his leaving the country. He yielded to their solicitations to remain, and the more readily that he had been requested by the Governor to favour him with his advice as to what was best to be done in the critical circumstances. A number of Europeans in Fort Beaufort, where he had resided after the destruction of his station, conveyed to him their wish that he should return and break to them the bread of life. He was most anxious to do so, but the war was still at its height, and the country between Grahamstown and Fort Beaufort was overrun by the enemy night and day, and consequently most dangerous. The outlet from the difficulty came from an unexpected quarter.

On the breaking out of hostilities, a body of converted Kafirs with their families had been settled by Mr. Calderwood at Fort Beaufort, under circumstances of considerable peril. When they came to know that he had decided to remain in the country, twelve of these men agreed to go and fetch their teacher and his family, if only they could be provided with the means of defending him and themselves from their own countrymen. The needful weapons were speedily forthcoming, and soon after they set off, travelling day and night, until in the early morning they had reached Mr. Calderwood's house in Grahamstown. On being asked how they had dared to come, they playfully said, "When we were coming for our father we were bold and strong; love has strong arms and long legs; make haste and come." Words these that deserve to be printed in letters of gold. Yet these very men, when first met with by Mr. Calderwood, a few years before, were naked savages!

Inquiring of Mrs. Calderwood as to what should be done, she joyfully responded, "Let us go at once; we can be ready to-day;" and by the afternoon they had taken the road. The journey, which occupied three days, was attended by many anxieties and perils. In particular, Mr. Calderwood was filled with the liveliest apprehensions, as at night-fall they began to descend a dangerous and uninviting pass, known as the Queen's Road—said pass being suggestive of the familiar lines in "The Lady of the Lake," in which, when Fitz-James is impatient to meet Roderick Dhu and his clan, that murderous chieftain is represented as suddenly calling his men from their ambush:—

> "Instant, through copse and heath, arose
> Bonnets and spears, and bended bows;
> On right, on left, above, below,
> Spring up at once the lurking foe;
>
> And every tuft of broom gives life
> To plaided warrior, armed for strife.
> That whistle garrisoned the glen

At once with full five hundred men,
As if the yawning hill to heaven
A subterranean host had given."

How he felt during the hours of darkness throughout that eventful night is best told in Mr. Calderwood's own words :—

"The emotions," he wrote, "which then agitated my breast, can never be described, and they can never be forgotten by me. As I walked by the side of the wagon containing all that was most dear to me on earth, I could only dimly see the countenances of our faithful escort. As I anxiously and hastily scanned them, their silent looks assured me that what man could do for me and mine would be done by them. My heart was too full to speak, and I could only lift it up to Him who hears even the groaning of the prisoner, when no words can be uttered. They read my feelings with the keenness of true affection. They spoke not, but pressed closer to the wagon, with their weapons in their hands, and by their intensely interested looks they seemed to say, in a way far more impressive than words could convey, 'If an enemy approaches you or this wagon, it must be over our bodies!' I felt almost ashamed of my anxiety, and all but ceased to fear. We reached our destination in safety."

The ride to and from Grahamstown was like that of Nehemiah, accompanied by his escort, from Shushan to Jerusalem, equally dangerous, and giving evidence of no small amount of courage, the outcome in the one case, as in the other of faith and trust in God. In both instances He who was thus trusted was as a wall of fire round about the travellers, bringing them through all dangers to their respective destinations in safety and peace.

It only remains to add that on Mr. Calderwood offering these brave fellows some money as a small token of his grateful appreciation of their praiseworthy conduct, they, with genuine feeling, declined it, saying, "Why should we take money from our teacher? What have you not done? What have you not suffered for and with us? You stood by us in danger. You have done for us far more than money can do. You have brought eternal life to us. We may not take money."

Let those who are in the habit of speaking or writing disparagingly of efforts to evangelize the natives of South Africa inwardly digest the simple facts just related. In the writer's opinion the history of professedly Christian lands furnishes few more touching exhibitions of unselfish and heroic devotion.

EMNYAMENI.

WITNESSES FOR CHRIST IN AN UNLIKELY PLACE.

"The wilderness and the solitary place shall be glad; and the desert shall rejoice, and blossom as the rose."—ISA. xxxv. 1.

"I give waters in the wilderness, and rivers in the desert, to give drink to My people, My chosen: the people which I formed for Myself, that they might set forth My praise."—ISA. xliii. 20, 21 (R.V.).

EMNYAMENI.

WITNESSES FOR CHRIST IN AN UNLIKELY PLACE.

ONE of the liveliest congregations in connection with the Burnshill Mission is that of Emnyameni, an out-station situated at a distance of eighteen miles from the central one. The road to it is through some of the grandest and most beautiful scenery in South Africa, reminding the traveller strongly of some parts of the Scottish Highlands. In particular, I may note the Booma Pass, a narrow, rocky gorge of the Keiskama, where a sanguinary conflict took place in connection with the war of 1846, between the Kafirs and the British, and in which may still be seen an inscription on a rock, commemorating the sad fate of the British soldiers who fell there on the occasion referred to. The district is a thoroughly hilly one, and for the last few miles the only mode of reaching Emnyameni, from the Burnshill side, is by walking, or on horseback, along a narrow bridle-path on the hillside, with awkward breaks here and there in continuity, necessitating the exercise of the utmost caution. To one like myself, unaccustomed to the saddle, the ride from the point at which the conveyance had to be left behind to await our return was not without its anxieties. But, thanks to a kind providence, and to the faithful horse, which, *though blind*, was said to be very sure-footed, knowing, as it did, every bit of the way, the few miles to and fro were accomplished without any mishap. One is reminded in this connection of Major Malan's experiences. In his "Rides in the Mission Field of South Africa" he writes: "I learned a lesson of faith during these gallops. The plains of South Africa are more or less full of large holes. In galloping you pass them every moment. The very large ones you can see and avoid. The smaller ones you cannot. Your horse, however, can see them; *and only keep your seat, and you are all right.*" Very true; but what in the case of a *blind* horse? More faith, the good Major would doubtless have replied. In the ride to Emnyameni, *fear*, rather than faith, it must be confessed, prevailed. My blind friend—blessings on him, if he is still alive—did his best to reduce that feeling to a minimum.

A more out-of-the-world, primitive place than Emnyameni can hardly be imagined. Yet there, with few external influences of a helpful nature, religion appears to flourish to an extent which in the circumstances could hardly have been looked for. Let the following illustrations suffice.

On one occasion, on going there to preach, the Rev. William Stuart, the missionary at Burnshill, found an unusually large number of *Red* (heathen) Kafirs assembled. Having inquired the cause, he was informed that on hearing of his intention to come and preach on the day in question, the Christian natives laid their heads together to arrange a feast, and had invited the *Reds* to share in it. And, as Robert Moffat once remarked, the natives of Africa "are always ready for a feast, whatever else they dislike." The preaching, of course, came first; the feast followed. This was taking the heathen by guile, showing a considerable knowledge of human nature on the part of the Christians.

When at Burnshill, in 1885, there appeared at the Mission House, one forenoon towards the end of the week, three young women, who had walked from Emnyameni, having started therefrom at break of day. They were in a very wet and draggled condition, for not only had somewhat heavy rain fallen by the way, but they had also forded three rivers—the Wolf River, the Keiskama at three different places, and another stream, the name of which has escaped me. They had come for the Burnshill Communion vessels for the ordinance to be observed at Emnyameni on the following Sabbath. After resting for an hour and a half, and getting some refreshment, they started on the return journey, thus accomplishing a walk of thirty-six miles in the course of the day, besides fording the rivers a second time. Before leaving the Mission House I had given each of them a small bright blue shawl, which did duty at church on the Communion Sabbath as an ornamental covering for the head. The trouble to which these young women put themselves in order to further the interests of the congregation of which they were members is worthy of all commendation.

Mr. Stuart and I, along with the native teacher, who accompanied us all the way on horseback, and might at home have been taken for an outrider, set out on the Sabbath morning for Emnyameni. On our reaching that distant station fully an hour after the usual time for service (having been unavoidably detained on the way), we found the entire congregation, including the heathen chief, waiting for us outside the church. Previous to going inside, the process of handshaking had to be gone through with them all—men, women, and children, including the *Reds*—and the heartiness of it was unmistakable. The same thing had to be repeated at the close of the service, which was a somewhat lengthened one, with a break of about half an hour in the middle. And not content with such expressions of interest, a number remained outside the native female teacher's hut,—in which we were hospitably served with a substantial repast, which reflected the utmost credit on her culinary arrangements,—their object being to give us a parting farewell after we had mounted our steeds for the homeward journey.

The entire services of the day were intensely interesting. The church was filled by as attentive and devout an audience as I have witnessed anywhere, either in Scotland or in Africa. The singing was in the genuine Kafir style—thoroughly hearty, if lacking somewhat in the artistic element. Mr. Stuart and I were the only whites present. Upwards of ninety took part in the ordinance of the Supper; and at Mr. Stuart's urgent request, the writer gave the post-Communion address, Mr. Stuart interpreting. What added to the interest of the proceedings was the baptism of three infant male Kafirs, all of whom, to their credit be it told, behaved splendidly, partly owing, perhaps, to the mothers being saved the irritating process of unrobing.

As we did not get away from Emnyameni until between four and five o'clock, darkness had closed in upon us before we were half-way to Burnshill, and it was of such a pitchy character that I was led in the course of the journey to ask Mr. Stuart how he managed to keep on the road, and was informed in reply that he was not driving at all, that the horse knew the road better than he did. The intense darkness, indeed, was advantageous rather than otherwise, as it gave me a grand opportunity of seeing the fire-flies, which were out in full force, causing a brilliant illumination. It was a new experience.

That Sabbath is numbered among the red-letter days in my African tour. And I have cause also to remember with gratitude to God His providential care, especially when crossing the rivers after the sun had gone down.

It is of interest to add that the chief referred to on page 51 afterwards embraced Christianity, and was publicly baptized, fully four years ago, at Burnshill, in the presence of a large congregation, as were also, subsequently, several of the younger members of his family.

SIKO ROLISISO.

INSUFFICIENCY OF THE RED BLANKET.

"I was well nigh in all evil."—PROV. v. 14 (R.V.).

"I thought on my ways, and turned my feet unto Thy testimonies."—PS. cxix. 59.

SIKO ROLISISO.

INSUFFICIENCY OF THE RED BLANKET.

SIKO was born at Peddie, and was the son of heathen parents, whose home in later years was at Emnyameni. As a boy he attended for several years the school at Burnshill, and lived for some time in the house of the estimable Mr. Laing, a former missionary in charge of that station. In 1861 Siko removed to Lovedale, attending the school classes for four years, after which he was entered as an apprentice in the blacksmith's department. While there, he was noted as a ringleader among those who opposed the truth, and when spoken to regarding his soul's interests, simply mocked. Early in 1868 it was found necessary to dismiss him, at least temporarily, for disorderly conduct, and for being a party to a serious fight.

On his return to Emnyameni, Siko donned the

red blanket, thinking, doubtless, that by again adopting this badge of heathenism he might secure himself against Christian influences. But the word of God is quick and powerful, and can pierce through a Kafir's blanket, even to the inmost recesses of the heart; or, as a Christian Kafir woman expressed it, "The Holy Ghost can work under the red clay."

Shortly after the arrival of Mr. and Mrs. Stuart at their field of labour, they visited, along with the other out-stations, that of Emnyameni, with the view of doing some evangelizing work, and took up their quarters at Siko's father's kraal. One day, in the absence of Mr. Stuart and the interpreter, some heathen gathered round the wagon; and as Mrs. Stuart was anxious to address a few words to them, she inquired if there was any one who could act as interpreter, when Siko stepped forward and volunteered his services. On her expressing surprise that he, a Red Kafir, should know English, he explained that he had been educated first at Burnshill, and then at Lovedale. Mrs. Stuart spoke seriously to him, referring specially to the account which one who had enjoyed such opportunities would have to give at the day of judgment.

The seed thus sown in soil that was beyond doubt unpropitious enough, by the missionary's wife, as well as by Mr. Laing, Mr. Govan, Mr. Mzimba, and others, of whom Siko ever after spoke with the greatest respect, bore speedily most precious fruit. For he soon found his way to the Mission House, joined the candidates' class, and was in due time received into the membership of the Church.

The reader may form some idea of the intensity of Siko's heathenism and opposition to gospel truth from the fact that when the Rev. Mpambani Mzimba, the native minister at Lovedale, heard of his conversion he held up his hands in amazement, and said that after Siko he would never despair of any one; while Siko himself, on being asked on one occasion how he felt when speaking mockingly of religion, replied, "The man inside was very sick and very bad sometimes." Poor fellow! he was afterwards accidentally and fatally wounded while hunting in the forest near his own home. He died after eight days of intense suffering, during which, as Mr. Stuart expressed it, "his Christianity shone forth clear as the noon-day sun." But indeed, from the day of his conversion his life had been in full harmony with his profession. So well was this recognised by the Christian people among whom he lived that they wished to elect him to a post of greater usefulness. But ere their wishes could be given effect to his heavenly Master called him to the higher service of the sanctuary above.

MBIKATA QONYIWEYO.

A TOILING LIFE AND A PEACEFUL DEATH.

"I am already being offered. . . . I have fought the good fight, I have finished the course, I have kept the faith: henceforth there is laid up for me the crown of righteousness."—2 TIM. iv. 6-8 (R.V.).

MBIKATA QONYIWEYO.

A TOILING LIFE AND A PEACEFUL DEATH.

THE following brief narrative is extracted from "Lovedale, Past and Present," and is inserted among these sketches as illustrating the beneficial effects of missionary labour.

"Mbikata Qonyiweyo was born near Berlin, King William's Town, in 1846. His parents were not Christians, and both died when he was comparatively young. He was never at school before coming to Lovedale, but taught himself so far, and could read the Kafir New Testament when he joined the school classes in September, 1873, at the age of twenty-seven. He knew nothing of English, and could not write. After being in school for ten months he became a wagon-maker's apprentice. In 1878, the fourth year of his engagement, he fell into bad health, and died of consumption. He left a legacy of five pounds to the native Church at Lovedale, of which he was a member. His character was that of a humble, conscientious Christian man, and he was esteemed by all who knew him."

The following notice of his death was published in the *Lovedale News*:—

"Mbikata Qonyiweyo died here on 17th March, 1878. He was well known to all at Lovedale. Those who knew him most intimately can testify to his thoroughly Christian character. He was one of those who offered to go to Livingstonia when the first call for men was made, and was one of the most regular at his post on Sundays in the work of visiting the kraals. In his note-book is a memorandum of a very interesting meeting in the Gaga, where there was a great interest created, and it is hoped some souls saved. His missionary, Rev. R. Ross, Toleni, Transkei, who had evidently watched him carefully, writes thus of him: 'His story is a touching one from beginning to end. I believe he has got rest at last. What a long fight he has had with the troubles of this world for twenty-two years, and a hard fight it was. A *tamba* boy, seeking food and a home

—a stable boy in the stables of the police of the Idutywa, seeking a livelihood—a herd boy among the farmers near Maclean—taken up and cruelly treated, and well-nigh killed on suspicion of having been the murderer of a Dutch child ; he is proved innocent and sent off a wanderer among the Transkei Fingoes, where he is received and kindly treated by one of the Christians ; here he stays working, and wishing to be fed with the crumbs that fall from the gospel and education tables of these Fingoes—his getting a very little education —his hearing and receiving the gospel, then admitted into the Church—his next movement to Fort Beaufort to earn money—then his return to the Transkei to make arrangements for entering Lovedale—waiting a considerable time in suspense, then getting a letter of introduction to Dr. Stewart—he is received, he stays, first as pupil, and then enters as an apprentice—works on for a time—then comes the end, and the words, "I am ready"—and dies peacefully.'"

ZIBI, THE AMATOLA CHIEF[1]

"Cast thy bread upon the waters: for thou shalt find it after many days. . . . In the morning sow thy seed, and in the evening withhold not thine hand: for thou knowest not which shall prosper, whether this or that, or whether they both shall be alike good."—ECCLES. xi. 1, 6 (R.V.).

ZIBI, THE AMATOLA CHIEF.

THE old Chief Zibi at Falconer, an out-station of the Burnshill Mission, about eight miles distant, was a great friend of the Rev. James Laing. He not only gave him substantial personal aid in the building of the church, but got his people to do so also. Nevertheless, he continued a red heathen to very near the end of his life. This was the more remarkable, seeing one of his wives and five of her children, including the eldest son, as well as a sister of Zibi's, had all of them become followers of Christ—the first of them as far back as 1858. He had thus been surrounded, as it were, for many years by a daily net-work of Christian influence, and the wonder is that he was able to hold out so long. A case such as his—and it is not an uncommon one—shows the terrible hold that heathen customs have over those who are under their pernicious sway, notwithstanding a measure of enlightenment.

Latterly, a marked change came over the old chief. When within a few months of his death Zibi showed much anxiety to converse on Divine things with Mr. Stuart, the present missionary, but he passed away without having given formal expression to his faith in Christ, and his acceptance of Him as His Saviour. The circumstances, however, attending his interment were remarkable, and lead one to indulge the confident hope that ere his departure he had been enabled to take shelter in the cleft of the Smitten Rock.

In connection with the interment of a chief, according to the usual practice, a deep hole is dug close by his kraal, and near the foot of it another opening is made, into which the naked body is placed in a sitting posture, along with his clothes, assegais, ornaments, and all else that he most highly valued when alive. All arrangements are made by the counsellors, and the chief cannot be buried otherwise without their consent. In the case under consideration, Zibi, contrary to expectation, was put into an ordinary wooden coffin, and buried in the Mission burying-ground in the presence of his counsellors, Mr. Stuart conducting a service at the grave, in which he was assisted by the Rev. Elijah Makiwané, of Macfarlan. Zibi's son and successor, who happily is a Christian, had no doubt something to do with the funeral arrangements. It is, however, more than probable that, when approaching his end, Zibi had not only fully consented to these, but had also given specific instructions regarding his interment, and that his counsellors, however they may have felt, did not dare to act contrary to his wishes. This is the more likely as Zibi had continued to the last friendly to the missionaries, and helpful to the cause of education, notwithstanding that Christianity had cost him several wives. The "great" wife left him for conscience sake, as he was living in sin with other women. So likewise did a second, who was the mother of his successor.

Zibi's widow was a *red* at the time of the chief's death, but the singular circumstance just narrated seemed to have been blessed to her. The morning after my arrival at Burnshill, in 1885, she turned up at the Candidates' class, to the great surprise of Mr. and Mrs. Stuart, and was in due course received into the membership of the Church. Not long afterwards she migrated to the Tora, in the Transkei territory, where Zibi's oldest son, also a Christian and an elder of the Church, resides. There she still lives and maintains her Christian character. One of Zibi's sons—Daniel by name—is spoken of as a very devoted Christian, a powerful speaker, and a successful worker.

Some, perhaps, may question the propriety of citing a case of the nature just described. Is it not possible that Zibi, and others in similar circumstances, without it may be even the dying thief's articulate confession, were while life remained translated from the kingdom of darkness into the kingdom of God's dear Son? Who shall dare to limit the Holy One of Israel in His gracious dealings with the children of men?

Mr. Laing, as well as his immediate successor, the godly and devoted Donald MacLeod, having predeceased the old chief, it was not given to these honoured missionaries to see even such fruit of their labours. But the time is coming when both sowers and reapers shall rejoice together.

CECILIA M. MSIKINYA.

A BRIGHT SUNSET.

"I drew them with cords of a man, with bands of love."—HOSEA xi. 4.

CECILIA M. MSIKINYA.

A BRIGHT SUNSET.

WHEN in South Africa in 1885, as I went from place to place, it interested me greatly to hear of the quite remarkable impression which the late Dr. A. N. Somerville, in the course of his tour in 1883, made upon Europeans and natives alike. His visit to Lovedale Mission Station was memorable not only as furnishing the opportunity for his opening the large hall of the new and noble Institution in the month of May of that year, but also and specially as the occasion for the sowing of seed which was destined to bear most blessed fruit.

It did so in one case at least—that of Cecilia Mary Msikinya, one of the older girls in the Female Institution, who, on account of her loveable nature, was a general favourite with the pupils, and who had distinguished herself by diligent and successful study. But up to the time of Dr. Somerville's visit, notwithstanding that the necessity of a personal interest in Christ had frequently been pressed upon her, as upon others, Cecilia withal knew not the Lord. Now, however, the time to favour her had come.

The subject of one of Dr. Somerville's addresses was the unrestful state of Noah's dove. In his usual felicitous and graphic way he described it fluttering round the outside of the ark. This was felt by Cecilia to be a picture of her own condition. Then the hand lovingly stretched out to draw the helpless bird to rest and peace told what the Saviour was waiting to do for her. It was enough :—

" So to the Ark she fled,
With weary, drooping head,
To seek for rest."

And she found it in Christ, for that very night she surrendered herself heart and soul to Him for forgiveness and salvation.

The new life then received was full of promise, and was solemnly and gladly laid on God's altar, to be devoted to work among the Red Kafirs,

Cecilia practically saying, in the lines by Richard Baxter,—

> "If life be long, I will be glad
> That I may long obey :
> If short, yet why should I be sad
> To rise to endless day ?"

It was not the will of Him who had so tenderly drawn her to Himself, that her life should be a prolonged one. The seeds of a disease which has slain its thousands had, by exposure to a wetting rain while resident at Healdtown, been laid in Cecilia's constitution, and slowly, but all too surely, it ran its fatal course.

During the long weary months of declining health Cecilia was tenderly cared for by the late Mrs. Muirhead, then the esteemed superintendent of that Institution, who from first to last had taken the deepest interest in all that concerned her bodily and spiritual welfare. On the occasion of my visit she told me the above-mentioned circumstances, and at her request I was very pleased to have the opportunity once and again of conversing with Cecilia. She greatly impressed me by her modest, subdued, and thoughtful manner. It seemed to be that of one who was living habitually under the influence of divine and eternal things.

Previous to my departure from Lovedale it had been arranged that Cecilia should go and reside, for a time at least, with her uncle, the Rev. David Msikinya, who was for some years a pupil and student of the Lovedale Institution, and at the time referred to was in charge of a Wesleyan mission station at Amatole, near King William's Town. It was hoped that the change might prove beneficial. This hope, alas! was not destined to be realized. When the time of her leaving drew near, the girls of the Institution were greatly affected—so much so, that it was thought better to keep them within doors when the actual departure occurred. Dr. Stewart having sent along his *spider*, Mrs. Muirhead and Cecilia drove off one pleasant June morning, after the doctor and I and one or two others had given the young invalid an affectionate and, as it proved, a final farewell. Cecilia, as was her wont, was wonderfully calm, and evidently did her utmost to restrain her pent-up feelings.

Though comfortably settled in her new quarters, and receiving from friendly hands every care and attention, Cecilia continued gradually to decline, and in the month of October of that same year passed peacefully away to her heavenly home, where all tears are for ever wiped away, and there is no more death, neither sorrow nor crying, nor any more pain. One is reminded by her case of those other lines,—

> " It is not death to die,
> To leave this weary road,
> And 'midst the brotherhood on high
> To be at home with God."

As Mrs. Muirhead expressed it in a letter to the writer, " it seemed mysterious that we should have to yield up our brightest and best. To Cecilia, however," as she further remarked, " it was but granting her own heart's desire ; for, as she said, ' to be with Christ is far better.' " Little did Mrs. Muirhead think when she penned these words, that she was so soon to follow her loved pupil to the better land :—

" EVEN SO, FATHER, FOR SO IT SEEMED GOOD IN THY SIGHT."

TOBY UNDAYI.

A RECORD OF FIFTY YEARS' SERVICE.

"Demetrius hath the witness of all men, and of the truth itself."—3 JOHN 12 (R.V.).

TOBY UNDAYI.

A RECORD OF FIFTY YEARS' SERVICE.

IT is the custom in the South African native Churches for the elders to take part in the devotional exercises, and even, in the absence of the missionary, to conduct the entire service; and though I did not understand what was said, the fluency and fervency of their prayers and addresses seldom failed to impress me. I was particularly struck with one of them when at Emgwali, perhaps the more so on account of its being the first occasion of my worshipping in a native church. On mentioning the matter to the Rev. Mr. Cumming, I was informed that the native referred to—the subject of this notice—besides being an old and consistent Christian, had also quite a remarkable gift of prayer. A sketch by Mr. Cumming of this estimable evangelist, who lately passed away, having appeared in the July number of the United Presbyterian Church *Missionary Record* for 1891, I am indebted to the editor for permission to include it in the present volume. The leading particulars were furnished to me on the occasion of my visit, but it is a satisfaction to be able to present them in this more complete narrative.

"The story," Mr. Cumming writes, "of Toby Undayi's conversion is remarkable. One of the bravest and most fearless of Tyali's young warriors, he wished, like other young Kafirs of his age, to get married, but had not the means. To procure these, he entered the colony by night, seized some horses, and returning, concealed them in the wood behind the Chumie school. On Sabbath morning he entered the church after the people had assembled for worship; and just as he entered, the Rev. William Chalmers read out the text, 'Thou shalt not steal.' The word pierced his heart, he stood confounded, wondering how the teacher could know what he had been doing. That night he returned the horses to the place whence he had taken them. Then he came to the teacher, confessed his sin, was received into the inquirer's class, and in due time into the Church, where his decision of character soon gained for him a leading influence among the people.

"In 1843 Toby was appointed to take charge of the station in Tembuland, left vacant by Mr. Cumming's removal elsewhere. There he laboured till the war of 1846 forced him to fly to Glenthorn, where Mr. Chalmers, Mr. Cumming, and a number of the native Christians had already found refuge. It was a time of sore trial, all the stations were destroyed, and Mr. Chalmers succumbed to the privations he had suffered. Toby refused to eat the bread of idleness during the season of waiting, and took a somewhat hazardous engagement as a shepherd, until the restoration of peace allowed him to resume work under Mr. Cumming at Chumie.

"The year 1850 brought upon Toby an accumulation of trials. War again broke out, plunging everything into confusion, and compelling the native Christians to seek safety at Peelton. While tarrying there, having lost all his goods and suffered many privations, he was called to lay his three children, one after another, in an early grave.

"Though thus 'written childless,' his faith endured in submission to the Divine will.

"Emgwali was in due time prepared for the fugitives, and in 1857 Messrs. Soga and Johnston opened the Mission station there, Mr. Johnston being succeeded after two years by Mr. John A. Chalmers. In 1861 Mr. Chalmers went to open Henderson Station in the midst of Anta's tribe, and Toby, mindful of the tie which had bound him to the father, followed the son to the new field. It was a wild country, a series of deep glens and precipitous mountains without roads, where missionary and evangelist found it laborious toil to reach the kraals high upon difficult heights, or remote in deep ravines. Their toil was crowned with early promise, a Church was formed and schools planted. But the promise was soon blighted. Mr. Brownlee, the Chief Commissioner, had by his high character and integrity exercised an admirable moral influence upon the district, and the disappointment occasioned to the tribes by his removal was deepened into resentment by their being placed under the control of his former clerk, who was quite a youth. Intimately connected with the removal of Mr. Brownlee was the refusal of Sandilli to comply with the wish of the Government that he should remove beyond the Kei river into the Galeka territory. The people felt they were no longer secure in their old territory, that their days in it were numbered; and, unhappily, they abandoned themselves to intemperance. Their drunken revels sometimes became like the orgies of demons. Often would Toby lift up his voice like a trumpet and warn the people amidst jeers and laughter to give up their evil ways and turn unto the Lord.

"Such a state of society could not continue long. In 1877 war broke out. The people were driven from their country. Henderson Station was burned, and the native Christians fled to Emgwali. The new governor, Sir Bartle Frere, proclaimed Emgwali a place of refuge for all loyally disposed Kafirs. Hundreds, thousands even, of homeless men, women, and children took advantage of the boon. A precious opportunity was thus given of sowing gospel seed among poor outcasts, by many of whom the sound of Jesus' name had never been heard. Many on the station, unaccustomed to teach, were stirred up to take part in the work, and throughout this special season of evangelistic labour Toby was in his element.

" When peace was restored, and the remaining Kafirs located in Galekaland, Emgwali was left like a garden in the midst of a desert. The school people alone were allowed to remain. The surrounding country was surveyed and divided into farms; these farms were soon occupied, and the farmers required servants. This opened up a new sphere of labour to Toby. He was appointed to visit these farms with the consent of the owners, and instruct the native servants as he had opportunity. At the first place to which he went the farmer at once consented, and added, pointing to a shed, 'There is a place for you to speak. I will call the people, and I will come myself with my wife and children, for we understand the Kafir tongue, and we shall hear what you have to say to them.' It was a trial to Toby, but he so spake, that when he was done, the farmer said, 'You may come here as often as you like. I have no fear of your stirring up the Kafirs against their masters. I will speak a good word for you to all my neighbours.' The same farmer afterwards said to Mr. Cumming, 'A better man than Toby, and a more honest Kafir I do not believe you have among all your station people.' Thus Toby, by the sincerity of his Christian character and bearing, overcame the strong prejudice prevailing among the farmers against the school people interfering with their servants, and opened for himself doors of usefulness.

"Tall, erect and spare, Toby moved about Emgwali, compelling by his firm and composed demeanour the respect even of those most prejudiced against the Kafirs, and welcomed wherever he was known. He was an acceptable preacher, a faithful and judicious elder, and a sympathetic friend to the suffering and the bereaved. As years advanced, the asthma, which had often added distress to the toil of his travels around Henderson Station, became very oppressive, and frequently laid him aside. At length he 'set his house in order,' and waited patiently for the desired change. His end was peace (this was in 1890). 'The memory of the wicked shall rot, but the righteous shall be held ni everlasting remembrance.'"

FERMA.

FROM THE ANT MOUND TO THE MISSION HOUSE.

" O Lord, truly I am Thy servant . . . Thou hast loosed my bonds. I will offer to Thee the sacrifice of thanksgiving."—Ps. cxvi. 16, 17.

FROM THE ANT MOUND TO THE MISSION HOUSE.

MANY bad things have been laid at the door of the Kafir, and not least, as already mentioned, that of ingratitude. This is certainly true, speaking generally, as regards the *heathen* Kafir. But when God by His Spirit changes the heart, old things pass away, and this evil characteristic with the rest, in measure at least. It did so, at all events, in one case that I came across.

Among those who joined the rebels in the last great war between the Kafirs and the British in 1877–78 were a Kafir and his four sons. The father was killed, and at the close of the war, when the rebel camp in the Pirie Bush was broken up, the four brothers tried to make good their escape. They found their way to the neighbourhood of Peelton, and were congratulating themselves that they had not been seen by any of the enemy. But they *were* seen by some soldiers, who fired upon them. One of the brothers was killed. Two of the others fled and made for the coast, which they reached in safety. A ball passed through the thigh of the fourth, making escape in his case all but impossible. This young man was in his eighteenth year, and bore the name of Ferma. Observing an empty ant mound close by, he managed to crawl into it, and there, undiscovered by the soldiers, when they came to see whether their shots had taken effect, he remained until darkness set in. Under cover of night he made his way, with the greatest difficulty, to the Mission House at Peelton, three miles off, and lying about ten miles from King William's Town, on the gentle slope of an undulating plain, bounded in the distance by a fine range of mountains.

The Rev. Mr. Birt, of the London Missionary Society, on learning that the wounded Kafir was one of the rebels, immediately wrote to the magistrate of the district, informing him of what had happened. In reply, he was requested to retain the rebel until the ball was extracted, and he had recovered from his wound, when the magistrate was to be again communicated with. This was accordingly done. After three months Ferma, who had been accommodated in the Mission House, having quite recovered, Mr. Birt wrote, as instructed, and was desired still to retain him until further advised. When I saw him in 1885, and again in 1887, no instructions had ever been received. During all those years Ferma was a trusted servant in Mr. Birt's family, as he still is, for anything I know to the contrary.

As soon as Ferma came into Mr. Birt's house in 1878, he showed an eager desire to learn, and gladly availed himself of help from all who were willing to teach him to read, etc. And so well did he profit by Mr. Birt's instructions that before a year had passed he had the satisfaction of baptizing him on a profession of his faith in Christ. Several years afterwards Mr. Birt and his family were arranging to go on a visit to England, and told Ferma that he would need to look out for another master. The young man was in great distress, and begged to be allowed to remain and take charge of the house during their absence.

To this proposal Mr. Birt consented, and on his return to Peelton he found that Ferma had done his duty most faithfully, house and garden being in the best of order.

Mr. Birt had repeatedly urged Ferma to accept of wages; but he, on each occasion, resolutely refused. It was not until a few years ago, when Ferma intimated his intention of getting married, that he was induced to take any, and even then it was with expressions of regret. Such was Ferma's gratitude.

There is perhaps no mission station in South Africa where more solid and successful work has been done than at Peelton. The appearance of the purely native village—with its broad and well-kept road, its tidy houses and garden plots, its large and handsome church, built almost entirely by the natives, and the well-conditioned appearance of the people—all convey the impression that the best of influences have been brought to bear upon it. This gratifying result is due to the lengthened and indefatigable labours of Mr. Birt, and to the excellent training which the girls receive in the Shaftesbury Home—an institution which, under Miss Sturrock's admirable management, is second to none in South Africa. Such as doubt the civilizing influence of Christian missions may advantageously pay a visit to Peelton.

NOTESSI JAZA.

SOWING BESIDE ALL WATERS.

"*God, that said, Light shall shine out of darkness, who shined in our hearts, to give the light of the knowledge of the glory of God in the face of Jesus Christ . . . We are pressed on every side, yet not straitened; perplexed, yet not unto despair; pursued, yet not forsaken; smitten down, yet not destroyed; always bearing about in the body the dying of Jesus, that the life also of Jesus may be manifested in our body.*"—2 COR. iv. 6–10 (R.V.).

NOTESSI JAZA.

SOWING BESIDE ALL WATERS.

BEING anxious to make out a brief visit to the Mission station at Main, in Tembuland, it was arranged that Mr. W. W. Anderson, one of the teachers in the Blythswood Institution, should drive me thither. It involved a journey of thirty miles over an undulating, treeless, pastoral district, which in 1885, owing to severe and long-continued drought, was in a very parched condition. As Main was not reached until about seven o'clock in the evening, and it was necessary that we should leave the following morning, shortly after ten, there was little time for seeing the people and the work. I had to be satisfied by attending the early morning prayer-meeting and shaking hands at the close with the native teacher, and such of the native elders and members as were present.

After breakfast, accompanied by the Rev. D. Doig Young and Mrs. Young, Dr. Weir, Mr. Anderson, and the native teacher, I had also the satisfaction of meeting and addressing Chief Vityi, with his wives and counsellors and some of his people, the native teacher interpreting. My remarks, though meant for all, were specially addressed to the chief, whose hand, after a good hearty shake, I continued to keep a hold of until I had finished. He listened very attentively, and when remonstrated with for his non-attendance at the services, and for not sending his children to school, readily admitted the truth of all that had been said, pleading by way of excuse that "the Tembu's head was hard." Notwithstanding promises made not only then, but at other times also, to Mr. Doig Young, this heathen chief, I regret to say, still clings to his heathenism. But prayer is being made for him without ceasing, and it cannot be doubted that he will yet become a trophy of Divine grace. Of this there is an earnest in the fact that one of his sons has been for some time past, with his father's consent, an inmate of the Mission House.[1]

[1] Since this was in type intimation has been made of Vityi's somewhat sudden death.

I would have liked much to have made the acquaintance of Notessi Jaza, the subject of this paper; but as, for the reason assigned, this could not be done, I am glad to be able to transfer from the Report of the Mission at Main for 1890, the sketch there given of her history. Mr. Doig Young writes :—

"Notessi's home was originally at Burnshill. While staying there no fewer than nine of her children died. Her husband died too—died a heathen. She at that time was a heathen also. Soon thereafter she removed to the Lovedale district, settling down at Gaga. While there the good seed which Mr. Laing had sown brought forth fruit. Notessi was converted.

"Thenceforward she set herself resolutely to put down all heathen customs. She gave herself also to prayer, so much so, that Nomatafa (wife of the Evangelist) said to her, 'I am a much older Christian than you; *but in prayer you are an example to me.* True, in your case the last shall be first.' Being the first in her village to become a Christian, she had to endure much persecution. But she was enabled to bear it all meekly.

"Though a widow and a grandmother she attended school and set herself to learn to read, that she might be able to read God's Word. And so earnestly did she apply herself, that by the end of a year she was able to read the New Testament. Then she at once began to hold prayer-meetings, and try to lead others to the Saviour. In that work she spared not herself, sowing the seed beside all waters. And God caused it to prosper; for a considerable number were led to Jesus by her.

"Notessi joined the Total Abstinence movement, and from the first she waged war against even what is called 'moderate drinking' of Kafir beer. She and a number of like-minded women advertised a meeting at Macfarlan on the Beer Question. Several young men who had been educated at Lovedale, hearing of this, took their Bibles to the meeting, boasting that they would soon close the mouth of these bold, uneducated women. But the young men themselves were silenced. And no fewer than twenty signed the pledge at the meeting.

"Though poor in this world's goods Notessi

found a way of obtaining some money to give to the cause of Christ. She often hired herself out just that she might get something to give. We remember a characteristic instance of this grace of giving. Having got ten shillings from a gentleman for certain valuable information as to medical plants, she at once, while looking at the half-sovereign in her hand, exclaimed, 'How good God is! I will now be able to give my yearly contribution to the Church.' And when she uttered this she was sadly in need of clothes for her body. But to the very last she always managed to give the promised contribution, at least six shillings a year, to the Presbytery's fund, besides something to the other funds; and her collector was able, after her death, to say that Notessi had no arrears for anything.

"Notessi was also very hospitable to strangers, and had a very warm heart to children. Almost every time we went to see her we found her surrounded by little children. And for a considerable time before her death she was in the habit of putting aside every day some milk for a little child that came regularly to drink it and fall asleep on her knee. Yet she needed that milk herself. And so one said to her one day, 'You need that milk yourself. Why do you give it to the child? Can her mother not get milk for her?' To which Notessi quickly answered, 'Her mother is not kind to her. And I think Jesus would like me to care for the little one.'

"During the few years Notessi spent at Main, she proved a valuable assistant as *Bible-woman*. Much precious seed was sown by her in the stubborn soil we met with in Tembuland. Her personal influence on fellow-Christians was great, and its fruit is still visible, very markedly indeed, in one or two that came into close contact with her.

"And now we have to record that Notessi has been called by the Master to serve in His temple above. She suffered much for a considerable time before the end came. But she bore all with Christian patience. Her faith was clear—never a shadow of a doubt crossed her mind. She loved to think of the affliction sent her as the process of polishing her for occupying her place in the spiritual temple above. Having no desire to stay, when one would speak as if she might be spared, and suggest special prayer for this, she would say, 'You may pray if you like; but I long to go home.' Jesus was with her. She knew it. She spoke of it. And now she is not here; because He has taken her home."

The secret of Notessi's contented, useful and happy life will be found in the verses prefixed to this sketch, and she herself might have expressed it in the words of the hymn:—

"Faith can sing through days of sorrow,
All will be well.
On our Father's love relying,
Jesus every need supplying,
Or in living or in dying,
All must be well."

TOLENI.

A FIELD WHICH THE LORD HATH BLESSED.

"And the word of the Lord was published throughout all the region."—Acts xiii. 49.

"He (Paul) went through Syria and Cilicia, confirming the churches."—xv. 41.

"So the churches were strengthened in the faith, and increased in number daily."—xvi. 5 (R.V.).

TOLENI.

A FIELD WHICH THE LORD HATH BLESSED.

REFERENCE has been made elsewhere to the mental capacity of the African. A remarkable instance of it will be found in the following narrative of a two weeks' evangelistic tour in the Toleni district of the Transkei, from the pen of Mr. John Knox Bokwe, of Lovedale, than whom the South African Church has few more intelligent and energetic members. The case referred to is the more noteworthy, inasmuch as it is that of a blind man, who labours in consequence under peculiar disadvantages.

The whole narrative is so full of interest, furnishes such a truthful and gratifying account of the mission work, and pays such a well-deserved tribute to the evangelistic energy and marked success of the Rev. Richard Ross, whose apostolic missionary career extends over a period of thirty-six years, that I make no apology for giving copious extracts from it in this volume; and I do so the more readily, having had the privilege of visiting the Toleni district, and knowing something of Mr. Ross's manifold and arduous labours there. Mr. Bokwe writes in the *Christian Express* :—

"Cunningham Mission Station, Toleni, Transkei, is the mother station of eleven or twelve preaching centres, under the ministry of the Rev. Richard Ross. Twenty-three years ago this station and the surrounding district were simply a wilderness. No church, no school-house, nor any other Christianizing or civilizing influence existed. In 1867 permission had been granted to the Fingoes in the colony to migrate across the Kei, and to occupy lands vacated by the Galeka Kafirs. Mr. Ross, son of one of the earliest missionaries sent to Kafirland, offered to resign his charge of the Lovedale congregation in order to follow them and found a new mission. It was, as may be supposed, uphill work, requiring much knowledge, faith, courage, and ability for hard work—continuous hard work. But as that energetic missionary possessed these qualities in abundance, his work prospered. Churches that were built as beacons of gospel light, some in places entirely surrounded by red heathens, are now full, and some have been twice or thrice enlarged. Schools are in vigorous operation. Blythswood and other like institutions in the Transkei have been established. Mr. Ross himself has traversed the land up and down, and knows Fingoland proper with a geographical accuracy that is most astonishing. He had, of course, a good deal to do with the formation of almost all that is known in the Free Church of Scotland's Foreign Mission Reports as 'The North Kafir Mission' from the river Kei to Tsolo, in East Griqualand. Under his own 'circuit' or parish there are now eleven churches, with twenty-six agents, of whom nineteen are school teachers. The number of elders and deacons is twenty-five; the communicants on the roll at the present time are about six hundred;[1] and the number admitted since the beginning of Cunningham Mission is about sixteen hundred in all.

"Mr. Ross has, unfortunately, broken down in

[1] Now about seven hundred.

health, and for eighteen or twenty months has not been able to leave his house and itinerate, as he continuously did during the rest of his thirty-four years in the mission field. Urgently feeling the want of this in his district, he last month sent a pressing request for help to the Rev. P. J. Mzimba, pastor of his old congregation at Lovedale, to come over with some of his people and help. When the matter came up before the Kirk-session, it was decided to accede to the invitation, and it was arranged that representatives should accompany Mr. Mzimba from the six stations of the Lovedale native congregation, where Mr. Ross started his work as a missionary, when he returned from college in 1856. The party consisted of elders and a small choir. The Deacon's Court voted a sum of money for road expenses, and a wagon and span of oxen were procured.

"On the 14th September we started, a company of fourteen, and reached Toleni on Saturday, the 19th, so as to begin services the next day. These we continued almost daily for a fortnight at one or other of the out-stations, and, I should say, we had the opportunity of addressing about 2,000 people during that time. At Toleni and Cegcuwana the Communion was dispensed, and there were baptisms of twelve adults and a large number of children.

* * * * *

" At all the meetings the Word was listened to very attentively, and at Ndakana we had the pleasure of witnessing several conversions, one of them being a young bride still in the enjoyment of her honeymoon. She was deep in red clay, and adorned with rings and beads, the usual heathen ornaments, from head to foot. Poor creature! she was greatly moved, and, weeping bitterly, asked what she was to do; she felt she was such a sinner. It was a touching sight, and almost the whole audience was moved. Many others expressed concern for their souls. We felt that at this place, and at other stations we visited, we had given ourselves too little time, being limited to only one day instead of two or three, which the people themselves desired, in order to have personal dealing and conversation with anxious inquirers, besides the formal addresses. We had to make the most of the 'two weeks' ere we returned to our homes in the colony.

* * * * *

"On the Communion Sabbath, September 27th, at Cegcuwana, there was among the infants baptized the child of a blind man. We noticed that at all the hymns the man joined in the singing, and was correctly repeating the verses of each hymn. On the Wednesday following, when we visited Govan, we met him again, and found that this was his regular station. It was another case of 'a man who was blind from his youth up,' whom God's Spirit had taught to see and know and follow Jesus Christ as his Saviour and Friend. He has a wonderful knowledge of the Scriptures, being able to repeat chapter after chapter, and as we found out afterwards, able to quote correctly from almost any book in the Bible. He is not absolutely blind, but sees only a glimmer of light, far from sufficient to read for himself. He has never been to school, except the school of God's Holy Spirit, who has opened his understanding, and sharpened his memory to a surprising degree. He is a fluent speaker, and the precentor in the

Govan church, and knows by heart nearly every hymn in the Kafir hymn-book. All his brothers are *red*, and, of the family, only his mother is a Christian. He has been blessed with a good wife a quiet, intelligent, and godly young woman, who reads to her husband passages of Scripture, and teaches him to recite them accurately, so that they are thus stored in this blind man's wonderful memory.

"As an instance, one of our number happened in speaking on the subject of intemperance, to quote a passage from Habakkuk. He gave the chapter right, but doubted whether the verse was the tenth. 'No,' said the blind man, 'the verse is the fifteenth.' He was quite right.

"Speaking of the wife of this blind man lead also to the remark that a very wholesome influence is being exercised by former pupils of Lovedale Girls' School, and members of the Lovedale Band of Hope, who have married in the stations we visited, also by another young mother who was educated at the Emgwali Girls' School, and joined in her girlhood the Rev. J. Davidson's blue ribbon army. We might also mention several cases of former pupils of Lovedale, and its branch, Blythswood Institution, who are taking the lead in doing good to others, and who, by industry and otherwise, are an example of what all should aim at when they leave school to work among their countrymen.

" Sizani Mpondo, teacher at Toleni, is a very industrious man, and has built a square house, and laid out a garden with fruit and other trees. He is one of the oldest native teachers in the country and while many have changed from one occupation to another, he has remained steadily devoted to school work for more than thirty years, and deserves the credit of having done good service to the Mission to which he belongs.

" Ndabakazi, an out-station four miles from Toleni, we had intended visiting on Monday, 21st September, and also seeing an old friend, Faleni Ngwabeni, who was a pupil at Lovedale for about eighteen months in 1874–75. Just as we were preparing to inspan in the morning news came that he had died the previous night. He was headman or chief of the Maduna clan in that district. By his kindness, gentle manners, and helpfulness to others, both Christian and *red*, rich and poor, he had endeared himself to his people. The school in his district was, through his influence, one of the best attended. He was a regular attendant at church, strict total abstainer, and one who led a perfectly moral life, except that he had two wives. We shall not easily forget the scene of mourning on that afternoon at the funeral of Ndabakazi.

"At Cegcuwana we met another Lovedale pupil, Campbell Kape, elder and evangelist of that district. He has a large square house of three or four rooms, and a well built round hut; cultivates very largely, his gardens being enclosed with a wire fence; has fruit trees and a vegetable garden; has taught himself shoemaking, and is continually busy. He is called by his neighbours 'a black Scotchman.' His wife is a fine Christian woman.

"At Govan our company was accommodated in a commodious, well-made hut, built of sods, with a wall two feet thick, and eight or nine feet high. It has three rooms, properly divided, each with its own door and window; a well-finished thatch roof; all the work, we were told, of a self-taught native workman. It was a well-conceived plan, and to my mind quite did away with the reproach that a Kafir hut is nothing better than a hovel. On inquiry, we found that, including material, it cost between £15 and £20, and is the property of Matthew Mgu, native evangelist at Govan. Both he and his wife are old pupils of Lovedale. The school teacher there, Alexander Nombebe, a Blythswood pupil, with his wife, a Lovedale pupil, are doing good work. ."

OLD DISCIPLES.

"They that are planted in the house of the Lord shall flourish in the courts of our God. They shall still bring forth fruit in old age."—Ps. xcii. 13, 14.

AMONG the Christians I met with in South Africa were many aged ones, but some of these, like Old Sutu, had not embraced Christianity until far advanced in life. Others of them, however, had done so in their early days. It is to these latter that the description "old disciples" properly applies, and the cases that follow may be accepted as specimens. The first that I came across was—

Nosutu Soga.

She was the mother of the Rev. Tiyo Soga, the first ordained Kafir minister.[1] Her husband was one of the chief counsellors of Gaika, and a somewhat remarkable man. Mrs. Soga was one of the fruits of the Chumie Mission in its

[1] An admirable memoir of Tiyo Soga was written by the late lamented Rev. John A. Chalmers, of Grahamstown.

earlier years. On becoming a Christian, notwithstanding that she was Soga's "great" wife, she felt it to be her duty to leave him, he being a polygamist with seven other wives. She remained, however, in the kraal, a lily among thorns.

When I visited Mrs. Soga in 1885 I found her in a hut adjoining the one occupied by Old Sutu. She was then upwards of eighty years of age, quite blind, and very feeble, but humbly trusting in the Saviour, whom for upwards of fifty years she had sought to follow. Since then she has been removed, her sightless eyeballs having been opened to 'see the King in His beauty, and the land that is very far off.' Her death was calm and peaceful; and the missionary at Emgwali testifies that during her last illness she repeatedly expressed her sense of the preciousness of Christ.

Shadrach Mgunana

was another "old disciple" whom I saw at Emgwali. He was a convert of the U.P. Mission, and the first elder of the native Church at that station. He was also father of Shradrach, one of four young men at Lovedale, whom Dr.

Stewart, in 1876, selected from among a number of other volunteers to go as agents of the Livingstonia Mission, and who died there after one year of faithful service.

For some time Mgunana's conduct had been such as to give just offence, and to necessitate the exercise of discipline; for, besides separating from his wife and family, he behaved otherwise in a manner entirely unbecoming his Christian profession. But in his case, as in that of other good men and true, who have similarly given the enemy cause to speak reproachfully, the Psalmist's words were made good, "Though he fall, he shall not be utterly cast down." He returned a penitent to his God, and to his sorrow-stricken wife, Tali, who received him in a truly Christian spirit, doing her utmost to forget the past, and to promote his soul's best interests, while he, on his part, gave unmistakable evidence to all around that he had been restored to his true character and position.

At the time of my visit Mgunana had considerably passed the allotted threescore and ten, and the statement made to me regarding him was that "his Kafir Bible was his constant study."

Going in unexpectedly one forenoon I found the worthy old Christian poring over its pages. Those other words of the Psalmist were strictly applicable to him: "Oh how love I Thy law! it is my meditation all the day."

Mgunana's wife predeceased him. After her lamented death his strength gradually declined, and towards the close of 1885 he passed away in the full hope of a blessed resurrection.

Mgunana's fall, grievous though it was, need not occasion surprise. One has but to remember the depths of heathenism from which he had been rescued, the workings of the old nature within him, the evil influences by which he was surrounded, and the absence of many of those restraints and safeguards which help to keep Christian people in professedly Christian lands in the right path, in order to the formation of a just judgment of a case such as his. He happily had heard and obeyed the word of Christ, "Go, and sin no more," and any who may be disposed to judge harshly of Mgunana, and such as he, would do well to recall that other word, "He that is without sin among you, let him first cast a stone at him."

A Father, Mother, and Son at Lovedale.

When at Lovedale I had the gratification of meeting with Tshuka, the youngest son of two of the early converts of the Mission. Before referring to his history, some particulars relating to his father and mother naturally take precedence.

When the Mission was established at Old Lovedale, in the Incehra valley, by the Rev. John Ross, in 1824, FITI, Tshuka's father, a kind of headman, was living as a heathen at a kraal in the neighbourhood. Almost immediately after the missionary's arrival he found his way to the station, and being very lame and hardly able to walk, he came daily on an ox, led by Tshuka, then about sixteen years of age. After a time the father, who was very friendly, took up his residence at Lovedale, and wrought on week days at his trade of blacksmith, in which he showed not a little ingenuity.

On the occasion of his baptism, in October, 1829, Fiti took the name of James MacKinlay, after Mrs. Ross's minister in Kilmarnock. When the war of 1835 broke out, being unable to accompany the Mission families in their sudden flight, Fiti betook himself to the bush, where he remained concealed for a considerable time. While in this retreat, in order to preserve a correct reckoning of the days of the week, with the view of keeping the Sabbath even by himself, he had recourse to a notched stick, on which he put a mark for the six ordinary days of the week, and a larger mark for the Sabbath. The said stick was afterwards sent to Scotland, and was for many years in the possession of the Rev. Duncan Macfarlan, of Renfrew, who took the deepest interest in the missions in Kafirland. During the time of his concealment in the bush Fiti saw one day a party of troops approaching, and being unable on account of his lameness to get out of their reach, he put his hand up to his eyes and engaged briefly in silent prayer. His prayer was answered; at all events the soldiers passed without observing him, and so the dreaded danger was averted.

Testimony was borne to the correctness of the old man's deportment, and to the progress he had made in his acquaintance with divine truth, as also to his faithfulness in reproving those who indulged in sinful practices, even though by so doing he should expose himself to persecution. He lived to a good old age, and died at New Lovedale about 1843.

Fiti's wife, NOBUYISWA, known by the name of Elizabeth, had also an interesting and in some respects a remarkable history. She was one of the first five converts baptized by the missionaries at the Chumie in 1823.

At her conversion Nobuyiswa came out very decidedly on the Lord's side, the change being deep and radical. She parted with her native ornaments and dress, of which she was well supplied, saying, "I have done with these things now; they belong to the old state. I must dress and live as one who has received the gospel."

Shortly after her husband's death, when about seventy-five years of age, Nobuyiswa lost her sight. The blindness continued for several years, when her sight suddenly returned, so that she could see thereafter with tolerable distinctness. Her other faculties, with the exception of that of memory, she preserved to the last.

Throughout her lengthened pilgrimage Nobuyiswa lived an eminently consistent Christian life, reproving sin wherever she met in with it, and pleading with the people to leave their heathen ways and throw in their lot with the followers of Christ. She died at Lovedale in 1868, being then over a hundred years of age. At the time of her death several of her great-grandchildren lived about her, while her great-great-grandchildren were with a daughter, then an old woman, further in the interior. The removal of such a well-known figure left a blank in the Lovedale district which was not soon filled up.

Tshuka

himself began life as a herd boy. In 1827, when about twenty years of age, this ardent young Kafir went with the mission wagon to Port Elizabeth to bring up the newly arrived missionaries, Messrs. Chalmers, Weir, Macdiarmid, etc., a distance of about 150 miles. He then became a regular wagon driver, and afterwards combined with that employment the occupation of quarryman. In this latter capacity he was at the formation of Pirie Station in 1830, and assisted at the building of the first wattle and daub Mission House. He quarried and carted all the stones, and aided in the erection of the more substantial house built in 1836. A similar service was performed in connection with the Manse at Old Lovedale about 1832, as also of the Church, Manse, and the first part of the original Seminary at New Lovedale between 1836 and 1840; and again when the Seminary was enlarged in 1855.

Nor was Tshuka's a half-hearted or eye service. For this testimony is borne of him, that while working as a quarryman he never had occasion to be on the outlook for his employer. On the contrary, though a day labourer, he worked conscientiously himself, and used his influence to secure as far as possible the same conscientiousness on the part of his fellow workmen.

Though Tshuka had been for many years under religious training, he was not admitted to the membership of the Church until about 1845. This happened some time subsequent to his marriage, and only after being faithfully spoken to on the subject by his friend Vimbe, an early convert and teacher of the Mission. About 1852 he was elected to the eldership when the first elders were ordained in connection with the native Church at Lovedale, and has been for many years the senior office-bearer there.

While engaged in quarrying during the week, Tshuka had acted as Mr. Weir's interpreter on Sabbaths. In this and in other ways he has rendered most valuable aid to the Lovedale Mission. He never had much education, though he had learned to read. His *forte* has never lain in the direction of books. He is nevertheless possessed of considerable individuality and independence of mind.

Tshuka was one of the speakers at the jubilee of the Lovedale Institution in July, 1891. On that occasion he spoke as follows:—

"My head is very old and unable to hold both all that is past and what is going on at present. I am going to tell you about the father of the young man (Mr. Weir) who laid this stone. I used to go out much with him to the Gaga and to places round about. At the Seven Kloofs there was an old and hardened Fingo who would not hearken to the Word of God. We often went to his place. One day, as we went to preach, I asked Mr. Weir this question, 'What are you trying to do? Why should you leave other people about the place, who are willing to hear, and worry yourself about this man who is so troublesome to us?' He replied, 'When a man has a garden, he does not neglect any part of it, but endeavours to cultivate it all. And he sometimes takes more trouble with the parts where the soil is harder and poorer. We are cultivating the soil.' I was satisfied. We were cultivating the soil. I specially remember an address that Mr. Weir gave to a few whom we got together one day in one of the kraals. It was on the words, 'Behold, He cometh with clouds, and every eye shall see Him.' I never went to this school (institution). I was not too old to learn, but some one had to work about the place, and I became the general pack-horse. I visited with wagons Graaf Reinet and Port Elizabeth on the business of the Institution, during times of drought and famine. I dug many of the stones that went to the building of the Seminary here. When they spoke about a Seminary, I asked what that was. Mr. Weir told me not to mind what it was, but to take my crowbar and dig the stones. He said I would learn in time what a Seminary meant. And so I did."

Tshuka is now in his eighty-fifth year, and nearly blind. He is one of the last remaining links with a somewhat remote past.[1] What changes have

[1] When this volume was first projected I resolved to dedicate it to the venerable Rev. W. R. Thomson, of Balfour, then the only remaining link among the European missionaries of a former generation. His death in May, 1891, in the 97th year of his age, precludes me from carrying out the purpose thus formed. His memory will be long revered in South Africa, as it is by me.

been witnessed during his lifetime—since 1824, when he came daily leading his father's ox at the founding by Messrs. Ross and Bennie of old Lovedale, then an unbroken waste of heathenism, until 1892, when the fruits of the labours of the intervening sixty-eight years may be seen in the noble institutions, with their 340 male and 203 female pupils; in the extensive industrial and boarding establishments; in the numerous substantial mission houses, and in the beautifully laid out avenues and gardens—the whole forming a scene such as is nowhere else to be found in Africa!

Noketilé,

better known at Pirie by the name of Helen, was among the oldest of "old disciples," and as notable as any of them. She was baptized at Old Lovedale, in Incehra Valley, as far back as 1827, while a servant with Mrs. Ross, the wife of the Rev. John Ross, from whom she took her name, to express her attachment to her mistress.

Noketilé's father resided in the neighbourhood of Joseph Williams's station, and was one of the first five converts who had been baptized and married according to regular Presbyterian form in connection with the Chumie Mission in June, 1823. He acted for some time as Mr. Bennie's interpreter.

Noketilé, the eldest daughter, belonged to a clever family, and was possessed of an excellent understanding. None of the people, it is said, excelled her in religious knowledge, and while still young the hope was cherished that it would prove in no ordinary degree fruitful in after years, which happily it did. From the time that she entered the service of Mrs. Ross until her death in 1888, a period of sixty-three years, her Christian life had been marked by a rare consistency. She was a constant reader of her Dutch Bible, and a most regular attender on the means of grace. Nor did her religion consist merely in such exercises. On the contrary, none were more exemplary in diligently discharging the duties of her humble station. In this respect, and on account of her Dorcas-like usefulness, she set an example alike to Christian and heathen.

It is not surprising that when considerably over eighty years of age Noketilé's faculties should have failed. The last time Dr. Bryce Ross spoke to her—he had known her ever since he could remember anything — she told him she had no wish to live any longer, as owing to her deafness she derived little benefit by attendance at church, while her blindness prevented her from reading her Bible. Hence the desire to depart. "But," she added, "I will patiently abide His time." She had not long to wait. Though not really ill on the occasion referred to, very soon afterwards her feeble frame succumbed after a few days' illness to the cold of winter, which is so trying to the natives even when in ordinary health and vigour.

Like Phœbe, Noketilé was "a servant of the Church, and a succourer of many." Yet would she have been ready to endorse the words of the hymn :—

> "Oh, to grace how great a debtor,
> Daily I'm constrained to be!"

Tombilé,

another convert of the Mission, is no less deserving of notice. The time and circumstances of her admission to Church membership are unknown. It appears, however, that in her early days she served in the family of the Rev. W. R. Thomson, of Balfour, and there is little doubt that while there her Christian life, if previously begun, as probably it had been, would be greatly strengthened.

In course of time Tombilé was married, and lived for some years with her husband in a part of the country remote from any Mission station. After his death it is believed she returned to her father's people, who were located at a Mission station. And at a later period, as her son, who had been educated at Lovedale, had become a teacher at Pirie, she went there to live with him. About 1867 she entered the family of Mrs. Bryce Ross; but by 1885, when I first saw her, she had retired from service.

Like Noketilé, Tombilé had maintained for a similarly lengthened period a consistent Christian walk. In speaking of her, Mrs. Ross said to me that "if ever there was a true Christian, Tombilé was one." Paul's desire for his Philippian converts was in an eminent degree fulfilled in her case—

"Blameless and harmless, . . . without rebuke in the midst of a crooked and perverse nation, among whom she shone as a light in the world holding forth the word of life."

Tombilé was very active in her habits. To the last, such was her youthful appearance, that though at the time of her death considerably over seventy years of age, any one who did not know the fact would not have taken her to be more than sixty. She might have been seen carrying on her head a large bundle of firewood from the forest, her house being a considerable distance from it. When I ascended Pirie mountain in company with a member of Dr. Ross's family and Miss Blair, Tombilé accompanied us, with right good-will carrying to near the summit a picnic basket, under the weight of which I for one would have groaned.

This ripe old Christian was suddenly laid prostrate by fever, under which, notwithstanding Dr. Ross's medical skill and his wife's careful nursing she soon succumbed. From the information supplied me by Dr. Ross shortly after, I gather the following particulars respecting Tombilé's last illness and funeral.

Mrs. Ross being anxious to read to her, inquired of Tombilé what portion she would like to hear. She answered, "The 15th of John." As the passage was being read her eyes brightened. Now and then she would put up her hand and make a remark. At the verse, "Abide in Me, and I in you," etc., she said, "Without Jesus we are nothing, without His help we can do nothing." Again, on the words, "Ye have not chosen Me, but I have chosen you," she raised her hand and exclaimed, "Yes, it is Christ from beginning to end; it is all His doing, not ours."

The funeral was the largest Dr. Ross had ever seen among the natives. At the grave, after reading several passages of Scripture, he addressed the large gathering of old and young, heathen and Christian, from the words, "The wicked is driven away in his wickedness, but the righteous hath hope in his death." The service was a most impressive one. Useful and fruitful as Tombilé's *life* had been, still more was accomplished by her death, insomuch that Dr. Ross was strongly reminded of Samson, of whom it is said, "So the dead whom he slew at his death were more than they whom he slew in his life." Previous to her death, some of her heathen neighbours went to her house to see how a Christian could meet death. And from what they saw and heard, the thought in their minds, though unexpressed, was doubtless in the case of some at least that to which Balaam gave utterance, "Let me die the death of the righteous, and let my last end be like his."

A SABBATH AT THE GORDON MEMORIAL MISSION.

COMMUNION AND BAPTISMAL SERVICES.

"A day in Thy courts is better than a thousand."—PSALM lxxxiv. 10.

"Jesus took bread, and blessed, and brake it: and He gave to the disciples, and said, Take, eat; this is My body. And He took a cup, and gave thanks, and gave to them, saying, Drink ye all of it; for this is My blood of the covenant, which is shed for many unto remission of sins." —MATT. xxvi. 26–28.

"And as they went on the way, they came unto a certain water; and the eunuch saith, Behold, here is water; what doth hinder me to be baptized? And he commanded the chariot to stand still; and they both went down into the water, both Philip and the eunuch; and he baptized him."—ACTS viii. 36–39 (R.V.).

A SABBATH AT THE GORDON MEMORIAL MISSION.

COMMUNION AND BAPTISMAL SERVICES.

IN 1887, through the kindness of Dr. and Mrs. Dalzell, I enjoyed the great privilege of spending three weeks at the Gordon Mission in the Umsinga district to the north of Natal. During that period I had abundant opportunities of seeing the work in its varied departments—pastoral, evangelistic, educational, medical, and industrial—in all of which there was much to interest.

In particular, Sabbath, 5th April, will not soon be forgotten. It was emphatically one of those red-letter days, of which so many fell to my lot in the course of my journeyings. On that occasion the Lord's Supper was observed by the infant congregation, when forty-four dusky Zulus, besides the members of the Mission staff, took part in the ordinance.[1] Specially interesting to me was the baptism of three children and eighteen adults (nine of each sex), the latter having been admitted to the ordinance after a more or less prolonged period of probation in the candidates' class, and very careful examination, not only by Dr. Dalzell, but also by the other members of the Mission staff, and qualified natives acting as office-bearers.

There were circumstances in connection with several of those then baptized which added much to the interest of the proceedings of the day, and which are deserving of special notice.

1. In August, 1882, a little girl from the Spandikron out-station, twenty-five miles distant from the Gordon Memorial, presented herself along with other candidates for baptism. Although pleased with her replies to the questions put, Dr. Dalzell did not see his way to baptize, on her own responsibility, a child apparently about eight years of age, and the only Christian in a heathen family. The reason for not acceding to her wishes was

[1] The number in full communion at the close of 1891 was 128.

carefully explained to her. She, however, had felt the disappointment much.

After her return home she continued her regular attendance at the services conducted by John Sibeya, the devoted native catechist in charge of that station, and spoke much to her father and mother of what she heard. By-and-by the parents were induced to go and hear also. The mother's heart was soon opened, and to a certain extent the father's too. He was interested, and got John to teach him to read, in order that he might be able to read the New Testament for himself. He made rapid progress, which was the more remarkable considering that he was a middle-aged man. His wife was behind him in this, but not in the more important matter of deciding for Christ. She gave her heart to the Lord, and desired to confess Him by baptism. The husband, on the other hand, while attending regularly the Sabbath services and sending the children to school, could not see his way to forsake the customs of the people. After waiting for him for some time, the wife, in January, 1885, came to the Gordon Memorial with her young daughter, asking for baptism. The mother was accepted without hesitation, but some were doubtful of the propriety of acceding to the girl's request. But after hearing John Sibeya's account of her consistent life, and considering that it was really through her influence that the mother had been brought in, Dr. Dalzell decided that she ought to be accepted. Accordingly, along with her mother and baby sister and little brother, she was baptized, and very happy she appears to have felt on getting the desire of her heart. Agreeably to native practice, she chose the name "Kezia," and her mother that of "Bethia." Their baptism, it may be added, was with the father's full approval.

In March, 1887, Kezia's father, who had continued his reading and attendance on John's preaching, was at the Gordon Memorial over a Sabbath. Dr. Dalzell preached in the forenoon on the Fall, dwelling specially on the words, "Adam, where art thou?" In the afternoon Mr. George Bruce, an artisan evangelist of the Mission (now at Overtown out-station), spoke from the words, "Remember now thy Creator in the days of thy youth," Dr. Dalzell interpreting in Zulu. A deep impression was produced, and several remained behind for conversation, Kezia's father being among the number. He then and there decided for Christ, and a fortnight later (5th April), with the other accepted candidates, was received into the membership of the Church. He chose to be named after me, a circumstance which I am free to confess added not a little to my interest in the proceedings.

I had repeated opportunities of seeing my namesake, as well as Kezia, and Mary, his eldest daughter (he has had nine or ten children), then a girl about seventeen, who had shortly before to leave service in a Boer's family in consequence of a spine curvature, and who, as the result largely of John Sibeya's instructions, was baptized in 1890. Mary's health gradually declined, and latterly consumption set in. The end came suddenly at the close of 1891, by the bursting of a blood vessel; but she was ready for the summons. Her mother, who came to the communion at the Gordon very shortly after the sad event, informed the friends there that her daughter "was peaceful and happy, quite glad to go to be with Jesus."

The eldest son of the family is still a heathen, but his young wife has declared herself a Christian, and will, it is hoped, be admitted to the fellowship of the Church, ere long, by baptism. This would be the fifth brought into the Church's fold from that family circle through the devoted labours of John Sibeya, aided, after her conversion, by the gentle and potent influence of little Kezia.

2. PHILIP, also a middle-aged man, had long been asking for baptism. The difficulty in his case arose from the circumstance of his being rather weak in the mind. He could not be taught to read, nor even to learn by heart texts from the Bible. But a lengthened probation had proved the sincerity of his profession. With beaming face, and even with tears, he had been heard to say, " I cannot learn in a book ; I cannot answer questions. My head is stupid ; but my heart learns. I do love Jesus. He died for me to take away my sins. I am a sinner. He is my Saviour. I do love Him." In view of such a profession of his faith there seemed to me, as to Dr. Dalzell and the native elders, who had given the case very earnest

consideration, no sufficient reason why this simple-hearted believer should not be admitted.

3. WILLIAM MITCHELL, then in his fifteenth year, and supported by a widow lady in England, was so named at her request in memory of her deceased husband. The youth's father died suddenly eight or nine years previously, just as he and his wife had resolved to confess themselves Christians and ask for baptism. William had been living in the Mission House occasionally, previous to his father's death, and for four years up to 1887, it had been his home. From his earliest years he had been characterized by a strong will and independent spirit, and even when very young was quite beyond his mother's control. In 1885 he applied for baptism ; but notwithstanding indications of a change, Dr. Dalzell told him he must prove his sincerity by his conduct. This, I am glad to say, he had done. The troublesome, sulky temper had been brought in good measure under control, and when an outbreak did occur, he was easily brought round, on its being explained to him that by such conduct he was grieving God.

Accordingly, when on the occasion referred to he again asked for baptism, it was with no little satisfaction that his desire was granted. It was touching to see his mother and sister, both of whom had been baptized some time before, welcoming him into the Church, as they joined in shaking by the hands the newly-baptized at the close of the service, and to hear the former say, " How my heart rejoices to-day ! "

According to native law as administered under British rule, William was the natural owner of both mother and sister ; and his becoming a Christian meant a good deal to *them.* It is to be hoped he will not fail in his duty towards them, that he will not disappoint their fondly cherished expectations, and that his strong will may stand him in good stead now that he has declared himself on the Lord's side. The last accounts received of William were that he had returned (in 1891) from Johannesberg, and was preparing a nice square house for his mother, sisters, and self.

My interest in the services of the day was not a little enhanced by the fact that I was not a mere spectator, but had been invited by Dr. Dalzell to act as an elder, handing the bread and the cup to the communicants, and holding the baptismal basin as the candidates, who stood in a kind of semicircle around the reading desk, had the water sprinkled on their heads in succession. The general appearance and decorum of the entire congregation was about all that could have been desired. The scene stood out in striking contrast to a large gathering of *heathen* natives which I had witnessed in the neighbourhood a few days before. Together the two assemblages formed a picture with its bright and dark sides, the recollection of which will remain as a lasting impression on the memory.

The services of the day were appropriately brought to a close by family worship in the Mission House, a number of hymns in English and Zulu being sung, and several of the fourteen male boarders—now numbering over thirty—taking part in the exercises.

The Mission, founded, and in great measure munificently maintained, by the Countess Dowager of Aberdeen and other members of the family, as a memorial of the Hon. James Gordon, has been for many years indebted also to J. Campbell

White, Esq., for most generous aid, more particularly in connection with the Overtoun out-station, under the charge of Mr. George Bruce, already referred to. The Mission, which is under the direction of the Foreign Missions Committee of the Free Church of Scotland, has in large measure surmounted its initial difficulties, and with the Divine blessing may be expected to exercise a powerful and most beneficial influence not only over the whole of the Umsinga district, but throughout Zululand as well.

ELIZA MALABASI.

AN UNEXPECTED REUNION.

"I will bring the blind by a way that they know not; in paths that they know not will I lead them; I will make darkness light before them, and crooked places straight. These things will I do, and I will not forsake them."—ISA. xlii. 16 (R.V.).

ELIZA MALABASI.

AN UNEXPECTED REUNION.

WHEN at the Gordon Mission I was taken by Dr. Dalzell to see in their own homes the various Christian natives living in the neighbourhood. Among those visited was Eliza Malabasi, the wife of Thomas Mabuya, a devoted catechist of the Mission. Instead of the usual Kafir hut with its *minimum* of furniture, I found Eliza occupying a substantial square-built stone house, with its two, if not three separate apartments, containing tables, chairs, bedsteads, timepiece, sewing machine, bookshelf, pictures on the wall, etc. It was a pleasing sight. I had noticed elsewhere, and especially at Peelton, in the Cape Colony, similar indications of the civilizing influences of Christianity, where, in addition to most of the articles above mentioned, my attention was arrested by the tastefully arranged and spotlessly snow-white window curtains in the house (also squarely built, etc.) of one of the native agents. These houses and the articles they contained were at once an evidence of the beneficial outcome of the Christian faith, and an educational training to the still heathen native. It is to be hoped that the day is not far distant when such houses, and such things as they bring in their train, will be general among the Christianized natives; but progress in this direction is necessarily slow. I was told, for example, that a native missionary had presented his father with a bedstead, mattress, etc., and that the first morning after it was put up the old man was found lying as before on the time-honoured mat on the floor! He greatly preferred what he had been accustomed to all his life to the new-fangled erection.

Eliza Malabasi's history is a remarkable one, justifying the remark that "truth is stranger than fiction." When a girl, she had been carried off from Zululand by some unprincipled Boers. Her mother followed the wagon for a considerable distance, crying, but they were deaf to her cries, and finally drove her away. After Malabasi had grown up, she was married, first to an Englishman, and then, subsequent to his death, to the catechist, already named.

It so happened that one who had been a patient at the Gordon Mission, on his return to his kraal in Zululand, shortly before the last Zulu war, spoke of Malabasi. An old woman was among the listeners, and pricking up her ears, said, "*That* was the name of her child. At the close of the war Malabasi, who had previously been communicated with on the subject, went and saw her mother, and brought her to the Gordon to live beside her. Thus, in the good providence of God, after a separation of forty years, mother and daughter were again reunited.

Malabasi carefully instructed her mother in the things pertaining to her soul's welfare, in which she was greatly helped by her like-minded husband. For a time they were very hopeful of good results, but by-and-by the old woman seemed to weary of their Christian home, and went to reside with a heathen son, elsewhere. It is disappointing, but the bread cast upon the waters may yet be found in answer to prayer.

HUNTER.

A FRUIT OF THE MEDICAL MISSION.

"Before I was afflicted I went astray; but now I observe Thy word."

"It is good for me that I have been afflicted, that I might learn Thy statutes."—Ps. cxix. 67, 71 (R.V.).

HUNTER.

A FRUIT OF THE MEDICAL MISSION.

NO department of mission work in South Africa interested me more than that of the medical. At all, or nearly all the stations which I visited, this formed more or less a marked feature in the operations of the Missions. It was to me particularly pleasing to witness every morning, between ten and twelve o'clock, six, ten, twenty, and in one or two instances even more, gathered at the Mission House to be examined and treated for some ailment. Only a very limited number of the missionaries have received a medical training, but all of them, by observation and experience, have acquired sufficient knowledge to enable them to prescribe for the less serious cases, and the natives are learning more and more to consult them, instead of the native doctors, who, though possessing, it may be, considerable knowledge of the medicinal herbs of the country, exercise, as a rule, a most baneful influence in many ways. The remarks of Mrs. Bishop, in her "Journeys in Persia and Kurdistan," may appropriately find a place here. She writes :—

"The Medical Mission is the outcome of the living teachings of our faith. I have now visited such missions in many parts of the world, and never saw one which was not healing, helping, blessing, softening prejudice, diminishing suffering, making an end of many of the cruelties which proceed from ignorance, restoring sight to the blind, limbs to the crippled, health to the sick ; telling, in every work of love and consecrated skill, of the infinite compassion of Him who came 'not to destroy men's lives, but to save them.'"

At the Gordon Mission I had special opportunities of noting the work in this department, not only on account of my lengthened stay there, but also because Dr. Dalzell is a fully qualified medical man as well as a missionary, and in consequence draws together, for advice and treatment, a large number from the surrounding district.

Among those who were in the small hospital while I was at that station, and whom I saw almost daily, was a young man named Hunter, from the region of Delagoa Bay. Towards the close of 1883 he was being conveyed south by an Englishman, along with a number of other natives, who had been engaged to work on the Natal railway. Being well supplied with tobacco, he had been in the habit of giving some of it freely to several of his companions, but when it was getting exhausted, he did not seem disposed to part with any more. One morning, while engaged in cooking breakfast, a fellow-countryman asked for a bit, and on its being refused he, in a sudden burst of temper, let fly the contents of the pot at Hunter, severely scalding one of his legs. Unable to proceed with the party, he was afterwards picked up by some good Samaritan, by whom he was taken to the magistrate, who sent him to the Gordon Mission, to be treated by Dr. Dalzell. The injury inflicted proved both somewhat serious and protracted. At the time of my visit, in 1887, he had been upwards of three years in the hospital, and the leg was still in a bad way.

During his lengthened stay in the hospital Hunter was, under the instructions of Dr. Dalzell and others connected with the Mission, brought to a knowledge of the truth, and baptized in July,

1885. On one occasion a companion asked him whether he was not very sorry at what had taken place, and that he was in consequence prevented from working. To which he replied, "No, I am not sorry, for if I had not got this bad leg, I might never have heard of Jesus." On another occasion some one said to him, "When you return home, won't you just fall back to your old heathen ways?" "No, I won't." "But your heathen friends will persecute you." "They may kill me," retorted Hunter, "but I will not give up following Christ."

Hunter was a short time in Maritzburg with the Rev. John Bruce, visiting the natives in the stores and kitchens. He afterwards returned to the Gordon Mission, and has since been engaged in evangelistic work there, taking charge of a small out-station.

THE BOER FARM MISSION IN NATAL.

"*And Peter opened his mouth, and said, Of a truth I perceive that God is no respecter of persons: but in every nation he that feareth Him, and worketh righteousness, is acceptable to Him. . . . While Peter yet spake these words, the Holy Ghost fell on all them which heard the word.*"—ACTS x. 34, 35, 44.

"*And the hand of the Lord was with them: and a great number that believed turned unto the Lord.*"—ACTS xi. 21 (R.V.).

FOR the last six or seven years special interest from a Christian point of view has attached to Umvoti county in connection with a revival of religion that has been in progress there among the Dutch farmers and their native servants. It is a stock-raising district on the central plateau of Natal, inhabited largely by Boers.

The name "Boer" is the Dutch for farmer—not to be confounded with the English word *Boor*—and was originally applied to border farmers, but in course of time it came to have a wider signification. It was the primitive Colonial Boers, who, being the first to travel to and colonize Natal, were known and spoken of as "Voor-trekkers."[1] According to Froude, "their adventures and ex-

[1] "Trekking" is the Dutch word for the nomad habit of moving from place to place.

ploits form one of the most singular chapters of modern history." It was in 1835-36, under the guidance of Louis Trichard, an old Albany farmer, Gert Maritz, a Graaf Reinet burgher, and Pieter Retief, a descendant of an old Huguenot family, that the emigration of the Boers from the Cape Colony commenced on an extensive scale. By the close of 1837 it is estimated that from 8,000 to 10,000, conveyed in upwards of 1,000 wagons, thus voluntarily expatriated themselves on account of the laws under which they lived, which, rightly or wrongly, they deemed oppressive: the generally harsh treatment to which they were subjected at the hands of the Colonial Government; the inadequate protection afforded them against the Kafirs, by whose continually recurring incursions their best farms had been laid waste; and from other causes. In all probability they had some real grievances. On the other hand, this great Trek can hardly be said to have been forced upon the Boers, trekking having been with them, as one has said, "an ingrained habit" for generations. In this instance I am disposed to think it originated rather in the restless desire to escape from British control. In any case, it was planned and carried out on a scale unknown before.

Consequent on the declaration of British sovereignty in Natal, in 1842, many of the Boers settled down in the country between the Drakensberg and the Orange rivers, and over the territory beyond the Vaal river, now known as the South African Republic—"the finest stretch of land in all South Africa." They carried with them, it must be said with regret, feelings of irreconcilable repugnance to the British Government, feelings which some of their leaders did their utmost to intensify, and which, to a large extent, continue to the present time to rankle in the minds of the people.

Sir Harry Smith, for several years, from 1848, High Commissioner, in an official despatch to the Secretary of State, described the peculiar characteristics of the Boers. They were, he said, men of strong prejudices, jealous to a degree of what they regard as their rights, and evincing a want of confidence in those by whom they are governed, but withal kind and hospitable, affectionate, grateful for kindness when convinced of its sincerity, and governed in the main by the dictates of morality and religion.

It was owing to an ignorant prejudice against the civilization of the natives by Christian missionaries that the Boers in 1743 compelled George Schmidt, the pioneer Moravian missionary at Bavian's Kloof (Genadendal), to leave the country. In 1816 they assumed a similarly hostile attitude, necessitating the issue by the Colonial Government of a peremptory order to the missionaries to return within the boundaries of the Colony. At a later date they expelled from the country north of the Vaal river Messrs. Inglis and Edwards, missionaries of the London Missionary Society, and also attacked and destroyed Dr. Livingstone's house at Kolobeng—a proceeding that had a direct and immediate bearing upon the exploration and opening up of Central Africa. Thus Livingstone wrote: "The Boers resolved to shut up the interior, and I determined to open the country; and we shall see who have been most successful in resolution—they or I."

To the foregoing description of the Boers it may be added that they are intensely conservative, especially in parts of the country far removed from towns, on the outskirts of civilization, where education and other liberalizing influences are at a discount. Though remarkable for their religious character and strict attention to religious duties, the pioneer trekkers, or Boers, yet grew up with little or no education, insomuch that "their moral condition was scarcely higher than that of the Hottentots or slaves, who were their household companions,"[1] leading General Imhoff, who made a journey into the interior in 1743, to report that if further neglected the people ran the risk of relapsing into barbarism. In course of time measures were adopted to remedy this state of things, and to promote their welfare.

Like the land from which they originally sprang, the Boers are entrenched, as it were, within the stone dykes of long-established customs, and stand in dread of anything that makes for progress, as the inhabitants of Holland do of the advancing tide, lest all that is worth possessing should be swept away. There are exceptions, but speaking

[1] "South Africa, Past and Present." By John Noble, Esq., p. 15.

generally, to all arguments that may be addressed to them in favour of change, it is enough for them to be able to reply that their fathers and grandfathers thought and did so. The following inscription on a tombstone in an English churchyard well expresses the sentiment of Dutch conservatism of the old school :—

> " He trod the paths his pious fathers trod,
> And loved established ways of serving God."

Some amusing illustrations of this conservatism were mentioned to me, but I shall not run the risk of offending my Dutch friends by reproducing them here, especially as, in consequence of their attention to the simple teaching of the Bible and the observances of the Dutch Reformed Church, they have, in the main, been distinguished for the maintenance of good order and morality.

When, in 1652, the Dutch East India Company took possession of Table Bay and occupied the lands skirting the foot of Table Mountain, the first act of Jan Anthony von Riebeck, the Governor of the settlement, was to hold a council of his officers, when the proceedings were commenced by supplicating the blessings of Heaven on the enterprise.

They prayed that "as they were called to the government of the affairs of the Cape of Good Hope . . . to maintain justice, and, if possible, to implant and propagate the true Reformed Christian doctrine amongst the wild and savage inhabitants, for the praise and honour of God, and the benefit of their employers, it might please the Almighty Father to preside at their Assembly, and with heavenly wisdom enlighten their hearts."

The social system of the Boers was based on that of the Israelites under the patriarchal dispensation. The natives they regarded as an inferior race, one of the fundamental laws of the constitution of the Transvaal, or South African Republic, for example, being that "the people will admit of no equality of persons of colour with white inhabitants, neither in State nor Church."

Until 1795, when the Cape Colony first passed into the hands of Britain, commercial life in South Africa had hardly any existence. In the hands of the Dutch East India Company it was for about a century and a half previous to that date a close monopoly. Nor was it only *commercial* repression; there was also repression of language. The

Huguenot refugees were allowed to remain in the Colony on the distinct understanding that "nothing but Dutch should be taught to the young, so that by this means French should entirely die out," which in point of fact it did before the close of last century.

But after all that can be said regarding the absence of progressive ideas, there is yet much in the character and life of the Dutch Boer that deserves commendation. Mr. John Fairbairn, one of the early Scottish settlers, and from 1824 to 1860 the able editor of the *Commercial Advertiser*, paid the following high tribute to the character of the Cape Dutch population: "For industry, loyalty, filial attachment, and all the feature virtues of a rising community, they would stand high in comparison with any nation on record. Their love of freedom also is strong and unquenchable, and their notion of it is simple and just. . . ."[1]

[1] Of Mr. Fairbairn it was said many years afterwards, by Mr. Porter, the Attorney-General of the Colony, and one of the ablest public servants the Cape Government ever had, that "he had done more than any other man living to raise the tone of thought and feeling all over South Africa." —"South Africa, Past and Present," p. 198.

Though disposed, as has already been said, to regard the natives as an inferior race, the majority of the Boers have all along been favourably inclined towards them, while not a few have been warmly interested in missions, readily placing their Hottentot or Kafir servants under missionary instruction. This has been more especially the case in recent years, missions having now a recognised place in the organization of the Dutch Church.

Thus much by way of introduction, and for the more intelligent appreciation of what follows.

I now proceed to give some particulars of the revival work alluded to in the opening sentence. And as in its earlier stages it was described by the Rev. James Scott, of Impolweni, I cannot do better than insert here the statement written by him fully five years ago.

"For some time," he wrote, "there have been rumours of a change going on amongst the Boers—a great quickening of their spiritual life. Our daily papers were last month full of letters grumbling that the annual races and other May festivities had been spoiled by the Boers refusing to join as usual with their neighbours, being too much taken up with prayer meetings.

"A nice native lad came from the farm of a Mr. P. J. Nel, and attended our school for a short time. After several letters had passed between Mr. Nel and myself in regard to the lad, and also about a teacher or evangelist to instruct his people (natives), I made up my mind to visit Mr. Nel. Starting from Melville (out-station), I took with me Thomas Sibisi; and after two hours of rough riding, we reached a Boer's house. The owner turned out to be a Mr. Van Rooyen, brother-in-law of the man we were going to see. Our reception was very cordial, and after a short rest we were directed on our way. Another two hours brought us to Mr. Nel's. I found he and his family understood English fairly well, so it was not necessary to try my rusty Dutch, which I had to do at his brother-in-law's.

"Mr. Nel and I spent the evening very pleasantly. He told me how he had been brought to see the need of the new birth,—how family bereavements had made him study his Bible; and how at last, some eighteen months ago, he had passed from death into life. Before that time, though a member of the Church, he had been a mere formalist. When he found the true peace, he could not but tell his neighbours; and to his delight he discovered that others had experienced the same change, and gradually the work of God's Spirit had spread till he could count some two hundred in his sparsely-peopled district who are rejoicing in the knowledge that their sins are forgiven. And now that they are in the light their hearts are touched to see the heathen perishing. He had spoken to his own servants, and some of them are anxious. . . .

"From Mr. Nel I heard further accounts of the work of grace having spread from the Boers to the natives living on their farms. I would much like to have visited all the places spoken of, but owing to a prior engagement could only visit Greytown, the county town, where, as I expected, I found the Rev. D. Russell, of Pietermaritzburg, holding a week of special services. In Greytown I met Mr. Nel's brother and others of those who have been quickened in spirit, and heard further accounts of the work amongst the natives. Thomas Sibisi and I gathered the natives together and had an interesting meeting with them : after which I joined Mr. Russell, who was preaching to a mixed Dutch and English congregation. After the service some thirty went into the inquirers' room ; while in the body of the church many earnest prayers were offered up in Dutch and English.

"On the following day, Saturday, I reluctantly turned homewards, sending Thomas to visit some of the farms where I had heard that the work of grace was going on. The report he has since brought is very encouraging.

"On my way home I halted at Mr. Van Rooyen's ; and as he is only some ten miles from Melville, I made arrangements that a preacher should be sent every fortnight. He was delighted, and promised to do his best to get the people together ; and, further, that he and his family would attend, and would give the largest place they had in which to hold the meetings.

"Most of the Boers understand the Zulu language well, so it is difficult to say where this may end. It is to me most encouraging ; nothing but seeing the work could ever have made me believe that the day would come when the Boer would trouble himself about the salvation of the Kafir. They are thoroughly at one with us, being Presbyterians."

The work just described continued to make

progress, and was altogether of so remarkable a character that the congregation of Greytown, of which the Rev. James Turnbull was then minister, would not admit that it was a revival, and insisted that it was rather life from the dead. Not only large numbers of grown-up people in Umvoti county professed to have been born again, but many children, some of them very young, according to the testimony of their parents, had found Christ. After a twelvemonth's experience Mr. Turnbull wrote that "the joy of whole households —fathers and mothers, grandfathers and grandmothers, with all their children, rejoicing in the love of God and in His grace shown to one and all —can only be felt when participated in." He added: "It is worth living other sixty years to see such another exodus from the house of bondage."

The members of the Greytown congregation had always been exemplary in respect of morality. They had been preserved from drunkenness and similar sins. Church attendance was fairly good. Many of the families maintained regular family worship, while in not a few cases there were not wanting indications of a living Christianity, though it failed in joyousness and aggressiveness. But the previously existing state of matters was entirely changed under the influence of this religious awakening—so much so, that some of the Colonial newspapers described it as "a religious fever," or "madness," and said that the people were in danger of starving, as they were not only giving up their usual amusements, but also abstaining from their ordinary work.

The interest excited ran chiefly in three channels: (1) In anxiety for the conversion of such of the congregation as there was reason to fear were members only in name, as well as of the children. In the three divisions of the county six prayer meetings were held every month—three for the younger, and three for the older people—some of the latter riding from ten to twenty miles to attend. At the meetings for the young people special notice was taken of the prayers of the children, some of the youngest having been the means of winning souls for Christ. This was one of the most striking peculiarities of the movement. Nor need it be matter of surprise to any that it should be so. Even a child can understand and accept the message of God's love as declared in John iii. 16, which, as one has said, contains the gospel in miniature.

(2) In earnest concern for the spiritual welfare of the Kafirs. Previously, little or nothing was done for them by the Boers. There were a few exceptions. In particular, a Mr. Brewer, an old elder of the Greytown Church, who for years previous to his death, nine or ten years ago, earnestly laboured for the salvation of his Kafir servant. It was when he (Mr. Brewer) was on his death-bed that the old Kafir yielded to his entreaties, and gave good hope that the message of the gospel had been received. But, as a rule, so long as the service for which Kafir servants were engaged was in any fair measure performed, their masters were content. Many of them, indeed, had grave doubts as to the possibility of making good Christians out of the natives—a doubt shared in to a considerable extent by the colonists—and, for the most part, seem to have thought it was no business of theirs to put the matter to the test. But no sooner had the grace of God begun to work effectually on the hearts of the Boers than

this scepticism was gone. They felt persuaded that what grace had done for them, it could do for the most degraded native. Accordingly, the Dutch farmers, who understand not only the Kafir language, but also Kafir nature, began to hold meetings with their servants, including their wives and children, reading and explaining the Scriptures to them, and engaging in prayer with and for them. But something more was necessary in order to follow up and give permanency to the movement. One of the most notable of these Boer families was that of Mr. Mias Botha. In response to an appeal made by him, the needed instrumentality was supplied in the first instance by Dr. Dalzell, of the Gordon Mission, in the person of Moses Mbeli, a Kafir preacher possessed of admirable preaching gifts, whose labours have been greatly blessed. He had been converted at the Diamond Fields, the result of reading a Bible which had fallen accidentally out of the pocket of a Basuto fellow-labourer, and at the very time that he was nursing his wrath against some one who was believed to have killed a relative. He was afterwards taught and trained by Dr. and Mrs. Dalzell.

This agent the Boers undertook to support. Singularly enough, his success at first was greatest at the farm of Mr. Brewer, already referred to. As there were upwards of a hundred converts—men, women, and children—the Greytown Kirk-session, acting under instructions from the Synod of the Dutch Church, on 27th July, 1887, formed them into a native congregation, forty-five adults having been baptized on that interesting occasion.

Messrs. Schoon and Dohne, Dutch ministers, Dr. Dalzell, Mr. Scott, and the Rev. John Bruce, of Maritzburg, visited Greytown on their way back from the Missionary Conference at Durban, in order to assist Mr. Turnbull in the baptism of the native converts. Miss Lorimer, who, along with Mrs. Dalzell, was also present, wrote that the service had been truly refreshing and cheering.

Reverting to the Boer family mentioned in the preceding page, Mrs. Botha, to the regret of all interested in the revival movement, died in 1889, and early in the present year Mr. Botha himself was removed by death, leaving behind him two sons and two daughters, all married, and, like their father and mother, earnest Christians. The whole family were converted in the course of ten days some seven years ago. Mr. Botha's removal is spoken of as a great loss to these and other relatives, as well as to the Church, of which he was such an honoured and useful member.

As the work advanced, several other native evangelists were supplied by various Missions, Mr. Scott, of Impolweni, being especially helpful in the matter.

"Amongst these evangelists," wrote Mr. Scott, "is one man, Petros Skosan, whose case is a striking fulfilment of the prophecy of Isaiah xi. This man's father was one of the regiment of Zulu warriors, who, in 1836, at a signal from that cruel tyrant, Dingaan, fell upon, and in cold blood murdered, in Dingaan's own palace, the Dutch leader, Retief, and all his party of about seventy men. The son is now an evangelist, supported by the descendants of these same Dutch Boers to preach the gospel of peace to his heathen fellow-countrymen. The father, who still lives, is also a member of the Church."

(3) The English residents in the county also shared in the blessing. The want of life among them had long been felt and deplored. To Mr. Turnbull it seemed a fitting opportunity that, when Dutch Boers and their Kafir servants were

pressing into the kingdom of God, something special should be done for his own countrymen. He was moved, therefore, to begin a week-night service for them, as well as a Bible reading for the children. In this he had the full sympathy of the Dutch congregation, and the hearty co-operation of Mr. Russell, of Maritzburg, who preached with much power in the large Dutch church day after day for fourteen days. Numerous conversions were the result, from 200 to 250 having entered the inquiry room. Nearly all of these belonged to the community of the Dutch Church. The movement, indeed, was, with few exceptions, confined at first to the Boers and their families. A Christian Association was formed in Greytown for strengthening the faith and quickening the love of the converts.

A few months previous to the formation of the native Church at Greytown, the district had been visited by the Rev. Andrew Murray, of Wellington, whose high-toned addresses, like all his published writings, did much to help forward the movement. Nor was the helpfulness of this honoured servant of God limited to Umvoti county. It was felt in the Umsinga district, further north, and indeed, more or less, among the various Dutch congregations in Natal visited by him in the course of his evangelistic tour.

Writing in November of that year, Miss Lorimer reported, as the outcome of his earnest words, "several very decided conversions" among the Umsinga Boers, the district in which her voluntary labours in connection with the Gordon Mission are carried on. The impression made by Mr. Murray's visit had gone on working like leaven, so that every now and then one and another were reported as being gathered in, and speaking to relatives and neighbours, and, like the Umvoti Boers, bethinking themselves of the natives on their farms. Thus mention was made in particular of three farmers who, until then, were strongly opposed to John Sibiya, the catechist at Spandikron, having meetings among the kraals on their farms, but at length begging him to come, and even calling together their Kafir servants and holding service with them themselves.

The interest in the Umsinga district continued to spread, insomuch that Dr. Dalzell was both delighted and grieved with the applications he received from the natives and their Boer masters—delighted at the spirit thus manifested, grieved that he had not a sufficient supply of teachers to send to them.

"One case worthy of mention," continues Mr. Scott, "is that of a woman who was brought into the light while her husband was on a journey far from home. He heard a rumour of what was going on, and started in a hurry for home, telling his friends that if his wife had taken up with these fanatics, he and she will soon separate. Within two days he and his wife were found with hands joined, praising God for His goodness in giving them such a blessed outpouring of the Holy Spirit."

When these sentences were penned the movement had been in progress for a period of three years, and at that time there were no fewer than fifteen preaching stations in Umvoti county, the station in each case being just the Boer's farm-house. Mr. Scott had, on more than one occasion, seen as many as eighty Boers, and from three to four hundred Zulus gathered together for worship, the services commencing on Saturday, and continuing, with brief intervals, until Monday afternoon.

Opinions vary as to the origin of this remarkable work. The Boers themselves trace it to a few of their number having been led to give more prayerful attention to the word of God. It only required a beginning, for, as in the case of similar revival movements elsewhere, "no sooner did one speak to his neighbour of the change which had come upon him or her than the reply came, 'Such also is my experience;' and ere long whole families were rejoicing together, and praying for their neighbours and kinsfolk.

The leading features of this revival bear a striking resemblance to that which occurred at Loch Tay-side and Glenlyon during 1816 and three following years, under the Rev. Robert Findlater, of Ardeonaig, and the Rev. Dr. John Macdonald, better known as the Apostle of the North. Thus, in the Memoir of Mr. Findlater it is recorded :—

"During the end of 1816 and the beginning of 1817 you could be at no loss, if you saw two or three persons talking together, to judge what the subject of their conversation might be, which was generally about some new acquaintance or relative brought under concern, how those under concern were coming on, or how others who were awakened found relief, etc. Such was the strong interest felt for one another, and for the progress of the work of conversion. Indeed, there were few families without one, and some families two or three, professing deep concern about the salvation of their souls. Matters continued so during the whole of spring, 1817" (p. 194).

"The inquiry was confined at first to *one* individual, who, for upwards of two years before, often walked alone over the hill of Lawers, in search of that spiritual pasture which he found more congenial to his taste and feelings. Finding another like-minded, they conversed together, and were encouraged to continue in their inquiry. Their example led others, in a short time, to 'go and see.' Ere long they formed an interesting group of young inquirers, 'asking the way to Zion with their faces thitherward'" (p. 300).

The course followed by those who have been furthering and superintending the movement has been very much along the lines indicated in the foregoing narrative. In view of the pastoral character of the district, it had not been thought desirable to form mission settlements, or to place the converts under a regularly ordained native minister, or even, for a time at least, to appoint a white superintendent. Until lately it was judged better to leave the Boer Farm Mission to a large extent in the hands of the people themselves, they doing all that was needful in the erection of necessary buildings in the neighbourhood of the various farms, and receiving from those interested such pecuniary and other help in the maintenance and guidance of the Kafir evangelists and teachers as circumstances might call for. It was intended, in short, that the Mission should be in closest harmony and sympathy, alike with the regularly constituted ministry and with the various mission stations, from which, indeed, the agents will be chiefly drawn.

The Rev. David Rossouw, who, since Mr. Turnbull's retirement to Cape Town, after long and valued service, has succeeded to the pastorate of the Dutch Church at Greytown, recently reported that the Boer Mission is being gradually organized on a firm basis. As it now stretches far and wide, and the Kafirs need a white man over them, Mr. Pieter Le Roux, who passed his examination before the Church Commission, was in January last appointed as a Missionary to superintend the work at the central and eleven out-stations. In this he is aided by three native evangelists and several young assistants.

Mr. Le Roux's special work will be the training of Zulu evangelists for the needs of Natal and the south-western parts of the Transvaal. This training school, which is now in operation, is the outcome of a suggestion made by the Rev. Andrew Murray, at a Ministers' Conference held at Utrecht, and, if well encouraged, as there is every reason to believe it will be, cannot fail by the Divine blessing to prove the most effectual means of securing the permanency of the work.

The salary of Mr. Le Roux is paid by the Dutch Church at Greytown; while one of the evangelists is supported by the Sunday Schools, another by the Young Men's Christian Association, and the third by the ladies of the congregation, each of the three to the extent of £18 per annum. This speaks well for the missionary interest of the congregation. Would that the liberality thus shown were more general throughout the Churches of South Africa, as well as elsewhere!

Mr. Rossouw testifies to the good feeling and growing spirit of liberality that prevail among the white people, as also to the signs of life apparent among the Zulus, thirty-two having.

during the past year, been baptized at one place; while at another, where there is no worker, a revival occurred, with the result that ten confessed their faith in Christ. He adds that at the present time a quiet but deep work goes on at the central station. These characteristic features afford the best guarantee of its steady growth and ultimate complete success, and are well fitted to encourage all who have the best interests of Boers and natives at heart to hasten by every means in their power the desired consummation.

There are, of course, hindrances of various kinds, such as the clinging to old habits and customs, living in badly built houses, the absence in many cases of suitable articles of clothing, Kafir beer-drinking and dances, and not a few among both white and black who directly or indirectly oppose the work. But as the revival movement advances, these pernicious influences are being gradually diminished.

The foregoing unvarnished narrative goes to show that as of old the Word of God is still quick and powerful, and sharper than any two-edged sword, and able to make wise unto salvation people of diverse nationalities, and that the blessing will not be withheld so long as the *subject-matter* of the preaching is "repentance towards God and faith towards our Lord Jesus Christ." As in the Loch Tay-side revival, "these and the various other doctrines connected with the Christian scheme of redemption were the subjects preached upon, and which God acknowledged, and will acknowledge, in every age of the Church, to the conversion of sinners, and the edification of the body of Christ." It appears further from the narrative that the Christian religion stands out conspicuously from all other religions as the only one that realizes the idea of a *common brotherhood*, making all, of whatever country, or colour, or class, who believe in Christ, to feel that they are ONE IN HIM.

THE LIQUOR TRAFFIC.

"Cast ye up, cast ye up, prepare the way, take up the stumblingblock out of the way of My people."—ISA. lvii. 14.

THE LIQUOR TRAFFIC.

IN order to estimate aright and with any degree of fairness the success attending missionary effort in South Africa, it is necessary to take into account the serious obstacles thrown in the way of its prosecution. The remark is not uncalled for, inasmuch as there are not wanting those who, either from an ignorant prejudice, or as the result of a too ready acceptance of insufficient, and consequently misleading statements obtained at second-hand, are inclined to belittle the work accomplished, and the difficulties against which it has had to contend. Yet are these difficulties of a very real and formidable nature, and that in no ordinary degree. I desire to fix attention on one of them—that of the LIQUOR TRAFFIC.

As is well known, *drink* is the supreme curse of South Africa. It is so to the white man there. Whatever may be thought of total abstinence in the general, it is unquestionably a great safeguard for inexperienced and unstable young men resident in the colonial towns, removed as they are from the good influences by which in many cases they were surrounded at home. I should rather say that young men who are not total abstainers run a terrible risk of being drawn into the vortex. For it is the testimony of all who have resided for any length of time in the Cape Colony or Natal, and have the best interests of the community at heart, that the towns along the South African coast, from Cape Town to Delagoa Bay, are strewn with the wreckage of human lives, through drink. Nor at the ports only, though there in greater abundance, but in many of the inland towns too, it may be seen.

So I find Arnold White writing[1]: "Nor let the intending Cape Colonist forget that if he means to be successful, he must abjure liquor. . . . A man who drinks in England will spell ruin for himself in South Africa."

One who has been in the colony nearly all his

[1] *Good Words* for 1886, p. 477.

life, and has travelled extensively through it, told me that when on a visit to Manchester, a lady made particular inquiry about a number of people who had lived in Pinetown. No fewer than five of these, he informed her, had to his certain knowledge, died from drink.

The case of three brothers, of which I was informed by the same friend, was peculiarly sad. One died through drink on the road in his wagon. The second dropped down dead in a canteen ; and the third, still alive for anything I know to the contrary, was some years ago a wealthy man, but at the time I heard of him (1887), he was a miserable broken-down drunkard.

Similar instances might be multiplied almost indefinitely. It is a lamentable fact, that young men in particular, destitute of a backbone of principle, fall an easy prey to the influences of the drink traffic.

But if the results of the traffic in the case of the white man are disastrous, they are far more terrible in their consequences to the native, because, on the one hand, to brew beer and other stimulating drinks for carousals has been with him for generations a universal practice, while on the other there is the absence of all power of self-restraint. Accordingly, when the white trader comes in with his rum, and gin, and brandy, they operate on the weak side of the African's nature with irresistible and deadly effect.

The canteens which are everywhere met with exercise a most demoralizing influence upon the natives. Thus Major Malan wrote twenty years ago: "That anything like a general improvement of the natives is possible, while canteens abound, may be doubted by those most deeply interested in their welfare."

The facts to be found in great abundance in official documents are irrefragible, and fully bear out the foregoing remarks. I cannot do better than quote some of them here. Thus the Resident Magistrate of Southeyville reported [1]:

"If the sale of brandy to the natives in the colony is not prevented or limited, their ultimate destruction as a people appears to me to be inevitable. Not less than twenty per cent. of the young men who go to the public

---

[1] Cape of Good Hope Blue Book on Native Affairs for 1880, p. 131.

works from this district return home, having acquired a taste for brandy. In most parts of the Transkei very many of the chiefs are confirmed drunkards, and it is only the want of an opportunity that prevents the greater number of natives from indulging in strong drink. The evils arising from the worst customs of the natives are not to be compared to those arising from the sale of brandy."

In the same Blue Book, p. 173, the special Magistrate of the Tamachà district reports as follows:—

"Drunkenness prevails, and is increasing to an alarming extent. Men, women, and even children, are rapidly becoming degraded and demoralized by their inordinate appetite for strong drinks. Death through drink is of frequent occurrence, and most of the crimes brought under my notice are to be traced to this cause. . . . There is scarcely a member of any of the principal families in the tribe who has not contracted this abominable vice, and in many instances their cattle and sheep, in fact, everything they possess, have been parted with in order to gratify their mad longing for brandy. It is not easy to suggest a practical remedy for this deplorable state of things, but increased supervision and the total prohibition of country canteen licenses adjacent to native locations would tend in some degree to mitigate the evil. . . ."

In consequence of the prevalence of Dutch ascendancy in the Cape Parliament favouring the trade in liquor, a bitter controversy raged for some time in connection with the sale of spirits to natives in the Transkei territory. This led to the appointment of a Government commission[1] in 1883, the report of which is a most valuable document. I extract from it the following passages:—

"The Commission has been deeply impressed with the emphatic and urgent representations contained in nearly all the evidence taken, and especially from the natives themselves, on the evils arising out of the sale and consumption of strong drinks. All this evidence points in the clearest way to the use of spirituous liquors (chiefly ardent spirits, the produce of the distilleries) as an unmitigated evil to the native races, and that no other cause or influence so directly increases idleness and crime, and is so completely destructive, not only of all progress or improvement, but even of the reasonable hope of any progress or improvement. Those members of the Commission who, for the

---

[1] The members of the Commission were: Sir J. D. Barry, Kt., Judge President of Eastern District Court; Hon. C. Brownlee, Chief Magistrate of Griqua Land East; W. B. Chalmers, Esq., Civil Commissioner and Resident Magistrate of the Stellenbosch Division; Rev. Dr. James Stewart, Principal of Lovedale Institution; W. E. Stanford, Esq., Magistrate of Engcobo, Tembuland; Hon. Thomas Upington, Q.C., M.L.A.; Jonathan Ayliff, Esq., M.L.A.; W. B. Berry, Esq., M.D.; E. S. Rolland, Esq., M.A.; Rich. Solomon, Esq., Barrister-at-law; John Noble, Esq., Secretary.

purpose of taking evidence, had occasion to visit the Border districts, were eye-witnesses of the mischief, wretchedness, and misery which multiplied facilities for the sale of spirits by licensed canteens in the neighbourhood of native locations are producing; if unchecked, it can only have one result, and that is the entire destruction of that portion of the natives who acquire the taste for brandy. All the better class of natives, and even the heathen and uneducated portion, appear to be conscious of this, and have implored the Commission to suppress the evil which is bringing ruin on themselves and their country.

"In the territories of Transkei and Griqua Land East, a prohibition of the sale of spirituous liquors to natives has heretofore existed and been enforced by law; and by clause 8 of the conditions of the Convention with the Tembus, under which the Tembus became British subjects, it is expressly stated that 'it is understood that Government will prohibit the sale of liquors to all natives'; and the Amagwate Chief, Dalasile, who for a time refused to come within the provisions of this Convention, but whose country now forms part of Tembuland, 'begged that the Government would strenuously prohibit the sale of brandy in his country.' The Government appear to have earnestly endeavoured to fulfil these conditions; and we find that when application was made for the appointment of a Licensing Board at Umtata, the under Secretary for Native Affairs, in addressing the Chief Magistrate, Major Elliot, in a letter dated 7th January, 1880, stated: 'It is important that the sale of spirits to natives should be prevented in every reasonable manner possible, and as a means to this end the Government would rather that no licenses for the sale of spirits should be granted. The Government, however, yields to the opinion you express as to the necessity for the sale to the Europeans, and consents to the issue of licenses for sale to this class of persons alone. As a means, and an effectual one, for preventing the sale to natives, care should be taken in the choice of men to whom licenses are given, and to secure this it is undesirable that they should be granted otherwise than by the Chief Magistrate, who will thus alone be accountable to the Government on this important matter. The effect of such prohibition has been and continues to be beneficial to the well-being of the natives, and helpful and necessary to the good government of the territories; and the Commission recommends the continuance of prohibitory law as provided for in sections 256 to 262 of the Native Territories Penal Code."

R. J. Dick, Esq., special magistrate, writing from King Williams Town on 12th January, 1886, thus reports:—

"Drunkenness has perceptibly abated during the year, but I regret to add, not from any improvement in the intemperate habits of the people, but in consequence of the want of means to purchase the poison with (owing to a severe and exceptionally long-continued drought). The inclination and appetite for drink merely lies like a smouldering fire at present, which the first faint breeze of returning prosperity is certain to fan into a raging flame. It is sad beyond measure to see this once splendid race slowly but surely declining and becoming more and more demoralized. . . . It is a short sighted and cruel act to allow canteens in the very heart of large native populations, where they are liable to neither supervision nor control. And that is pretty much the condition of nearly all the canteens in the proclaimed areas. I am confident that I express the prayer of over 30,000 souls when I pray the Government not to revive the canteens already closed, nor to consent to the removal of the restrictions now in force. In the *total prohibition* of the sale of liquor to natives lies the future welfare and prosperity of the black races, and although the question is surrounded with difficulties, I sincerely trust the day is not far distant when it will become an accomplished fact.[1]

Again, Lorenzo Boyes, Esq., C.C., writing from the Magistrate's Office, Somerset East, on 7th January, 1886, states :—

"There is not the slightest doubt in my mind, after thirty-one years' experience, that brandy should be kept out of the way of the native as much as possible, and not put in his way by having canteens all over the country. I am aware that there is an aversion to the so-called class legislation, but still hope to see it carried into effect some day, as at the present time the natives are not sufficiently advanced to be able to discriminate between the use and abuses of alcohol. I have always found drunkenness to be the root of all the crime and immorality prevalent among the natives of this colony."[2]

One more extract I am tempted to submit. It is from the "charge" of the Bishop of Cape Town at the opening of the eighth synod of the diocese of Cape Town in 1887 :—

[1] Blue Book on Native Affairs, 1886, p. 31.

[2] Same Blue Book, p. 52.

"The principal hindrances to Church progress which are reported to me," said the Bishop, "are ignorance and a low standard of morality amongst our people, with the inevitable accompaniment of the shockingly prevalent vice of intemperance. And here I cannot omit to utter in the strongest terms I am capable of using my vehement protest against the action of our legislature in the last two sessions, first, in repealing the excise duty, and secondly, in removing the restrictions against the sale of liquors to the native races within certain defined areas in the eastern part of the colony. If the native races were acknowledged to be the natural enemy of the white man, and if the great aim of the latter were to exterminate the former, it is difficult to see what more successful action could be taken than that which has been taken by the legislature in the last few years. The natives even pray us to withdraw an almost irresistible temptation from them; and our reply is to make brandy cheaper, and to remove these restrictions to their obtaining it which have previously existed."

It is surely unnecessary to indulge in any reflections on the facts here submitted. I would only run the risk of weakening their force were I to do so. Suffice it to say that no more potent adverse influence is felt by all who put their hand to missionary work than the traffic that has been so strongly condemned by authorities whose judgment cannot be gainsaid. It is *the* great stumbling-block checking the onward progress of the gospel chariot in South Africa.

CONCLUSION.

"There remaineth yet very much land to be possessed."—JOSH. xiii. 1.

"Speak unto the children of Israel, that they go forward."—EXOD. xiv. 15.

CONCLUSION.

According to the Divine Word, "Ethiopia shall soon stretch out her hands unto God." If it be asked, how? I answer, in supplication—in *helpless* supplication (Isa. xlv. 14, and Zeph. iii. 10). And if any do inquire further as to the nature or terms of the supplication, is it not in substance, if not in so many words, the Macedonian cry, "Come over and help us"? Nor is it Ethiopia only that is now seen stretching out her hands, but AFRICA in its entire length and breadth makes its appeal. And the appeal should come with all the greater force to the Churches of Britain and America, in view of the centuries of neglect that has been the lot of "the dark continent," the deep moral degradation in which the natives have been and still are sunk, and the cruel wrongs inflicted on them for generations in connection with the accursed slave trade.

It will not do to make the imperfections of the Christianized Kafir, of which so much is heard in certain quarters, an excuse for leaving the native in a state of barbarism. As if, forsooth! with any show of reason he could be expected to reach perfection at one bound. The Rev. C. W. Kilbon, of the American Mission in Natal, in a paper read at the Missionary Conference held at Durban, in 1891, justly said :—

"Before we judge, let us reflect that these people have had the torpor of heathenism to overcome, the mind to awaken to perceive, the energies to arouse to act, and that in all their hereditary habits no attention whatever has been paid to the cultivation of a sense of moral obligation before God; the main end of life has been to serve the chief, and to gratify animal instincts. We should remember that they have had among themselves none of the uplifting helps that we grow up with,—no worthy ideals, no elevating public sentiment, no high minded leaders, no literature, no societies for mutual improvement, no refining influences generally, and few restraining and upbuilding laws adapted to their progressive condition. . . . If any are disposed to blame for the slow progress made, let the weight of their condemnation rest on the Satanic forces that have so effectually paralyzed the race."

If there are still those who doubt the practicability of raising the African to a level with the

English-speaking race, either the wish is father to the thought, or men must shut their eyes and ears to the plainest and most incontrovertible facts. The much-lamented SAMUEL A. CROWTHER, once a slave boy, and for twenty-seven years Bishop of the Niger, whose high culture, distinguished administrative abilities, and eminently successful efforts for well-nigh half a century to advance the material, moral, and spiritual well-being of the natives, marked him out as among the greatest benefactors of the African race; TIYO SOGA, the first ordained minister to the Kafirs, and, in the words of the *Cape Argus*, "to all intents and purposes a perfect gentleman . . . eloquent in speech and keen in thought," whose translation of the "Pilgrim's Progress" so competent an authority as the late Hon. Charles Brownlee pronounced to be "a perfect masterpiece of easy idiomatic writing," and whose lamented death at the early age of forty-two was felt by colonists and natives alike as a great public loss; VELDTMAN, whose sterling common sense, general intelligence, more particularly on educational questions, and loyalty to the British Government, have secured for him a recognised place as the leading headman in Fingoland, and made him influential for good among his fellow-countrymen; JOHN KNOX BOKWE, a Kafir by birth, at once a specimen and fruit of the Lovedale Mission, who for upwards of twenty years has been most usefully employed in the office there, during the greater part of the time as book-keeper and cashier, and whose musical gifts, knowledge of telegraphy, business habits, "energy, reflection, and sound judgment," have in the estimation of Dr. Stewart, as well as of others who have come in contact with him, "rendered him a very valuable agent in connection with the complicated work of the place;"[1] these and many other natives of similar stamp are a standing proof of their mental capacity. Let any one who is inclined to be sceptical on the point visit the Lovedale Institution, and he will find there young men from various parts of Africa who are in good measure able to hold their own with those of other and more highly favoured nationalities. It is not a matter of opinion, but of fact, the proof of

[1] See Appendix.

which may be found in the Government Blue Books, which are accessible to all.

I do not say that even the highest type of African—say the Kafir or Zulu-Kafir, taken at his best—is at present equal in all respects to the European or American, especially in Anglo-Saxon energy and perseverance. *I only assert his capability under favourable influences.* Time must be allowed in order that his mental and moral nature may fully recover from the deadening effects exercised on it by centuries of ignorance and oppression. Possibly the fruits of the educative process now in partial operation will not be seen even in the children's children of the present generation. But the inherent power in the South African of advancing in the social scale may well encourage all sections of the Christian Church to the adoption of energetic measures for raising him from the low marshy level of a degrading heathenism to the higher and purer planes of Christian civilization. What is needed there, as elsewhere, is the strengthening of existing agencies in the first instance, and their extension or multiplication, according as the needful means are provided, in order that the land may be more completely taken possession of for Christ. But even now, notwithstanding limited resources in men and means, and in spite of serious hindrances thrown in the way of missionary labour, in connection especially with the wide-spread and demoralising traffic in intoxicating liquor, a point has been reached whence a hopeful survey can be made.

I lately came across a speech of the Rev. Canon Scott Holland (Canon of St. Paul's), who presided at one of the meetings on the occasion of a recent anniversary (1891) of the Universities Mission. After referring in an interesting and forcible manner to the beginnings of Christianity in England, as narrated by Dr. Bright in his "Early History of England," his closing words were:—

"After a thousand years another Dr. Bright may write that Chancy Naples[1] came to this spot and built a church of reeds. Take Dr. Bright's 'Early History of England,' just read it, gather up the pictures which he presents to you with all his force and power, and say: 'I am present at a scene like this. The issues of Africa are being decided; I can hear how it is done; I can be present at these little scenes

---

[1] One of the Universities Missionaries then present.

where everything looks so small, and yet from which everything which is so great will issue hereafter; I am working with God in the great unrolling of this scene in Africa.' "

The foregoing quotation has been introduced for the encouragement of all who are engaged in laying the foundations of the Church of Christ in Africa. In the estimation of unfriendly critics the work accomplished may appear contemptible and barren of results, or at least altogether inadequate in view of the labour and money expended, and, as regards Western and Central Africa, the still more precious lives that have fallen on the field. Even the labourers themselves may be tempted to under-estimate its importance and to feel sometimes as if they were beating the air. Let it however never be forgotten by such that their great work is that of sowing the seed—the incorruptible seed of the Word, "which liveth and abideth for ever." The fructifying process may be slow: in many cases the fruit is not reaped until after the sower has passed away. But He who has said, "My Word shall not return unto Me void," will see sooner or later that the promise is made good. Even now, along with foundation work, which the scattering of the seed in large measure is, there are not wanting indications of growth, the precursors of a glorious future. In addition to those presented in the foregoing pages, take a further illustration from the Burnshill Station. When started, the first meeting-place for worship was under a tree, then in a round hut, then in a little square building, now or lately used as a wagon-shed, then in a somewhat larger stone church, with thatched roof, still used as a school, and *now* in a more substantial and commodious building, capable of accommodating about six hundred.

The same process of enlargement and growth has been and still is in operation all over Africa —the spiritual equally with the material—and it will continue to go on until the desolations of many generations have all been repaired, and in view of an accomplished work, as regards the establishment of Christ's kingdom there, " He "— the CHRIST, whose work from first to last it is, of whom in the prophecy Zerubbabel is the type— " *He* shall bring forth the head-stone thereof, with shoutings, crying, GRACE, GRACE UNTO IT."

APPENDIX.

IN confirmation of the statement made on pages 208–11, with respect to the mental capability of the African, a few extracts from an address in August, 1891, by Mr. John Knox Bokwe, as chairman at a meeting of the Lovedale Literary Society, may appropriately be reproduced here. His remarks on the occasion embody the testimony of an intelligent native, and show of what stuff he is made. Having glanced, retrospectively, at the condition of the natives, looking at the subject both on its bright and its dark side, and after giving expression to some thoughts bearing on personal influence, literature, and civilization, Mr. Bokwe proceeded :—

"That Christianity is spreading is evident, though perhaps not so much the genuine acceptance as the influence of it. I can tell of many a Christian home ; I have seen and heard of many a Christian death ; of many a young man and young woman drawn from evil to good. The blessings of Christian marriage are being realized. The immoral tone of heathenism, though still very dreadful, is improving, or at least hiding itself somewhat out of sight. A sense of shame is beginning to prevail, though you who come from Europe with pure eyes and more sensitive feelings may hardly perceive it. The warlike spirit has gone ; in its place may be seen a quickening passion for knowledge, a singular strengthening of brotherhood. The people are more sensitive to wrong, more slow to anger.

"You blame us for being lazy, but it is better to be even lazy at work, than not to work at all. That is a fault that will mend. The fact that men and women work without the need of anger and the rod is a great stride. Work is slow in this country. Even Europeans have developed a proneness to take things more easily than in their own country.

"Christianity is making itself felt, and it is the most powerful influence of all—the influence that searches deepest into the hearts of men. The natives, as a rule, have no serious objection to it. I believe that if the Christian faith is persistently and earnestly put to even the darkest of our heathen, it will be found that the only drawback to its acceptance is the love of sinful ways and customs, to which they cling most tenaciously. They are at least willing to listen, and I feel sure in their better moments willing to believe . . ."

INDEX.

Butler & Tanner, The Selwood Printing Works, Frome and London.

www.ingramcontent.com/pod-product-compliance
Lightning Source LLC
Chambersburg PA
CBHW030119030726
47498CB00007B/2450

* 9 7 8 3 7 4 2 8 1 0 6 3 2 *